PRAISE FOR *CAMP AVERAGE*

"Hilarious, irreverent, and timely, highly recommended for sports fans, summer-camp alums, and preteen-year survivors."
—*Kirkus Reviews*, STARRED REVIEW

"A wild and wacky novel…that will delight young readers who want to relive their own camp experiences or summer camp wannabes."
—*The Globe and Mail*

"A fun summer read. "
—*Booklist*

"A great book about friendship and standing up for what you believe."
—*Pennsylvania School Librarians Association Teaching and Learning Literature Review*

"This is definitely one book you'll want to pack in your duffel for summer reading."
—Sally's Bookshelf blog

For my parents

Text © 2020 Craig Battle

Owlkids Books acknowledges the financial support of the Canada Council for the Arts, the Ontario Arts Council, the Government of Canada through the Canada Book Fund (CBF) and the Government of Ontario through the Ontario Creates Book Initiative for our publishing activities.

Published in Canada by
Owlkids Books Inc.
1 Eglinton Avenue East
Toronto, ON M4P 3A1

Published in the United States by
Owlkids Books Inc.
1700 Fourth Street
Berkeley, CA 94710

Library of Congress Control Number: 2019947241

Library and Archives Canada Cataloguing in Publication
Title: Camp Average, double foul / Craig Battle.
Other titles: Double foul
Names: Battle, Craig, 1980- author.
Identifiers: Canadiana 20190143045 | ISBN 9781771473095 (hardcover)
Classification: LCC PS8603.A878 C37 2020 | DDC jC813/.6—dc23

Edited by Sarah Howden
Cover design by Alisa Baldwin
Cover illustration by Josh Holinaty

Manufactured in Altona, MB, Canada, in December 2019, by Friesens
Job # 259420

A   B   C   D   E   F

ONTARIO ARTS COUNCIL
CONSEIL DES ARTS DE L'ONTARIO
an Ontario government agency
un organisme du gouvernement de l'Ontario

Canada Council
for the Arts

Conseil des Arts
du Canada

Canadä

Publisher of Chirp, Chickadee and OWL
www.owlkidsbooks.com

Owlkids Books is a division of bayard canada

CAMP AVERAGE
DOUBLE FOUL

CRAIG BATTLE

Owlkids Books

TABLE OF CONTENTS

CHAPTER
1

"GUILTY AS CHARGED"

Mackenzie Jones had seen this look on his friend's face before. It was the bottom of the ninth of the All-Camp Junior Baseball Tournament final, and Andre Jennings stood in the batter's box, his jaw clenched, eyes narrowed, and nostrils flared. The look usually indicated that something special was about to happen. That is, if the pitch would ever arrive.

"Now I see why they have a pitch clock in the major leagues," said Miles Holley, shifting nervously next to Mack. "This is taking forever."

Andre's bright white jersey read "Camp Avalon" across the front, but the kids who went there never called it that. As far as they were concerned, they attended Camp Average, the least competitive sports camp in the world.

"The pitcher's just trying to psych Andre out," Mack replied to his friend. "It's a classic Killington move."

Known for its baseball dominance, Camp Killington

had won every All-Camp Tournament for more than thirty years—until the previous summer, when Andre, Mack, Miles, and a bunch of their friends had pulled off a minor miracle and put an end to the streak.

But the Killington kids were so sure they'd win the rematch this year that they let Camp Average host the final on their senior-camp diamond for the second straight summer. And now Andre was trying to prove them wrong. He just needed a ball to cross the plate.

"Okay, pitcher," the umpire said finally. "Let's play ball."

The pitcher, a skinny kid with a long ponytail and killer changeup, nodded at the ump and grinned at Andre. He wound up and delivered a low fastball.

BANG!

Andre smacked the ball high over the pitcher's head. Killington's center fielder tracked it in the air and slowly moved back, back, back … until he bumped into the wooden outfield fence with a thud. A second later the ball landed well beyond it, and the fans in the bleachers beyond first base jumped to their feet. They stomped and cheered, high-fiving in their orange camp T-shirts.

"Nice one, Andre!" shouted Winston Smith, their junior camp director from the summer before. As always, he was dressed in a light gray hoodie, red short shorts, knee-high white socks, and black old-school running shoes.

Mack cast the director a quick sideways glance, then returned his attention to the field to see Andre tap his foot on home plate.

The home run made the score 4–1.

For Killington.

Despite Andre's obvious greatness at the plate and on the mound, the famous baseball camp would not be denied this year. A few minutes and three outs later, the game was over and Killington had reclaimed the coveted trophy.

Mack and Miles stood to clap for their team's efforts and took a step onto the field ... from the bleachers.

The summer before, Winston had thrown a major curveball of his own by rewriting the campers' schedules and making competitive sports mandatory. That meant Mack and Miles got drafted onto the baseball team even though they'd signed up for other things, and Mack had responded by organizing a camp-wide revolt. The epic battle ended in a stalemate, with Mack and Winston each getting only part of what they'd wanted.

But this year, to Mack's relief, there had been more than enough participants for all competitive sports. So he and Miles—now twelve years old and in their last summer as junior campers—had gone back to their first loves: water sports and rocketry, respectively.

On the diamond, Andre, a tall, athletic boy with dark

skin and black hair, pulled his green-and-yellow Oakland A's cap low over his eyes and left the dugout to congratulate the winning team. Mack watched his friend shuffle through the handshake line until one of the Killington players grabbed his hand tightly, stopping him in place. The boy was even taller than Andre and had broader shoulders than any coach on the field.

"Deets," Mack whispered under his breath.

Terry Dietrich was baseball royalty because of both what he could do on the field and who he was related to. His uncle was Jeffrey Dietrich, the former Major League Baseball star whose talent had solidified Killington's baseball reputation. Around these parts, Terry went by his uncle's nickname, Deets, and he was so good no one would ever tell him he didn't deserve it.

"What's he saying?" Mack asked no one in particular as Deets leaned in close to whisper something to Andre.

Miles squinted through his glasses at the two boys holding up the handshake line. "I might be seeing things, but it looks like he said, 'There's always a pot of stew at Killington.' Is he offering him lunch? Is that a baseball thing?"

Mack eyed his friend skeptically.

"Okay, maybe I need to revisit my lip-reading book," Miles conceded.

As Andre finally pulled away from Deets to continue on down the row, two other Camp Average players finished slapping hands and bumping fists, and made a beeline for Mack and Miles.

"We're number two—again!" yelled a smiling Patrick Meyer, the team's starting catcher, with right fielder Nelson Ramos in tow. "We're number two—again!"

"You can stop chanting that now, Pat." Nelson winced at the sound of the slightly updated unofficial camp slogan. "We got the point two weeks ago."

"Hey, never let a good joke die, New Money," Pat replied, using Nelson's camp nickname. "And besides, is it not still accurate, despite all the changes?"

After the baseball team's big win the year before, Camp Average became the most talked-about sports camp in the area. As soon as summer was over, Winston got promoted to overall director and started in with his modifications. He'd created two streams for campers: "competitive," for kids who wanted to be challenged athletically, and "other," for kids who didn't want to be challenged at all.

Enrolment skyrocketed. When the current summer started, every available spot was filled with elite athletic clay for Winston and his coaches to mold.

The only problem? The molding hadn't yielded results.

None of the teams facing off against other camps had had any major success—not in ball hockey, golf, tennis, or anything else. The junior baseball team had made the tournament final, but that was as good as things had got.

"Well, we're not *all* number two," Miles challenged Pat. "The girls' teams are definitely number one."

Pat laughed. "That's only because they have no one to play!"

Winston had recognized that there was a lack of options for elite girl athletes in the area. And that had led to his other major off-season move: building a new row of cabins and opening Camp Average to girls for the first time ever.

But despite the talent the girls' teams showed, that same lack of options meant they had no one to pit themselves against.

"That may be true," Mack told Pat, "but don't let Nicole hear you talk like that."

"Talk like what?" a voice asked.

The boys turned to see Nicole Yen, Mack and Miles's friend from back home, approaching from the other end of the bleachers with her pal Makayla Munroe. In previous years, both had gone to Camp Clearwater across the lake, but they'd jumped at the chance to spend the summer playing basketball, softball, and ball hockey at a place with better coaches and facilities.

"Oh, hey, Nicole! Hi, Makayla." Miles reddened. "We weren't saying anything."

"Funny," Nicole pressed, "because it seemed like you were saying the girls' teams deserve the same reputation as the boys' before we even get a chance to prove ourselves."

"And what reputation do the boys' teams have?" said Andre, finally arriving on the scene and dropping his gear onto the ground by the bleachers.

Mack closed his eyes tight and rubbed his brow.

"Oh, I don't know," she said. "Maybe the reputation of proudly shouting about being number two."

"Guilty as charged," Pat said before Andre gave him a withering stare.

"Yeah, we shout that," Andre said, returning his attention to Nicole, "but we won the baseball tournament last summer. We get to shout whatever we like."

Nicole rolled her eyes. "That makes as much sense as calling your tournament 'all-camp' when you don't even include Clearwater."

"First of all, it's not *our* tournament. It's been running since before we were born," Andre protested. "And second, does Clearwater even have a baseball program?"

"Well, no." Nicole blushed. "We don't … *didn't* have any competitive programs. But it still would've been nice to be asked."

Mack put his thumb and index finger in his mouth and whistled loudly, drawing focus away from the fight. "I knew it was a bad idea to leave the waterfront!" he shouted at the sky. Then he turned to his friends. "Andre, you played a great game, and you don't have to fight a stupid fight started by Pat."

"That's right!" Pat shouted. "You're getting in the way of my one-liners!"

"And, Nicole," Mack continued, "Pat didn't mean any harm. Well, he did, but no more than he inflicts on the rest of us all day long. He's just trying to get under your skin."

Nicole looked at Pat. "True," he admitted.

"We all know you 'competitive' kids care only about winning now—which I still don't understand. Like, there's a speedboat and water skis literally a five-minute walk from here," Mack added. "And I mean, why spend all school year stuck in class listening to adults, only to come to summer camp and listen to adults?"

"Mack! You're losing your train of thought!" Miles shouted, bringing him back to Earth.

"The point is, you're not competing against *each other*!" Mack blurted. "Can we be cool?"

Nicole took a deep breath. "You're right," she said. Then she addressed Andre. "I'm sorry. Good game. That homer was awesome."

"Thanks," Andre replied. "I'm sorry, too. And hey, I'm as bummed as you are that you guys don't have anybody to play. I'm sure you'd do great."

Nicole broke into a cocky grin and threw her arm around Makayla's neck. "So are we!"

"Man," Nelson said when the dust had finally settled, "if this is how *we're* handling all this losing, Winston must be *dying*."

Right, Mack thought, conjuring up an image of the man known as much for his obsession with winning as for his red short shorts. *Winston*. With everything going on in the aftermath of the game, Mack hadn't even seen him leave the field.

Which, Mack thought, wasn't all that unusual these days.

Over the first three weeks of camp, he and Winston had avoided each other completely. Mack wasn't part of the competitive stream and therefore didn't need to worry about the fate of those teams. He did what he wanted when he wanted, and he went days without thinking of the camp director at all. It was bliss.

While Nelson had a point—the mounting losses must

have been taking a toll, and a miserable Winston was a desperate Winston—Mack was determined to stay out of it.

"Ah," he said, brushing off the idea with a wave of his hand, "I'm sure he's fine."

CHAPTER 2

"WE GET IT—WE'RE MONSTERS!"

"Heads up!"

It was 7:00 a.m., a half hour before breakfast, when a soccer ball flew off Mike Triplett's hockey stick and through the air of cabin 13. It gave Andre's brush cut a brush cut as it careened toward the plain brown plywood wall at the front of the room. Mike's twin brother, Spike, tried to head the spinning ball in midair, but he whiffed, stumbled, and landed on Miles in his lower bunk.

The ball hit the front wall and dropped into the hands of Brian, cabin 13's head counselor, who was sitting on his bed by the door.

"Nice …" Mike started.

"… catch!" Spike finished.

"Guys!" Brian yelled. "How many times do I have to tell you? If you're going to play soccey indoors, no slap shots. Keep it to wristers or saucer passes. You're going to take someone's head off!"

"Or get whistled for high-sticking!" Mack chimed in, trying to sound indignant.

"In actual fact," Miles said, climbing out from underneath Spike to inspect the model rocket he'd been fiddling with before getting tackled, "high-sticking is not in the soccey rule book. But it might be enforced under the catch-all rule Laker added last year, which was, and I quote, 'If anyone hits me with a stick, so help me ...'"

"I never thought I'd say this, but I miss Laker," Mack said of their former counselor and baseball coach. When Winston became camp director, Laker had been promoted to head baseball director and the solo cabin that came with the gig.

"Hey, I take offense at that," said Hassan, their newly certified junior counselor, who was dozing on his bed at the back of the room. He had helped coach the baseball team the summer before, so the boys knew him well. "Don't make me regret taking the assignment no one else was brave enough to accept!"

"Okay, okay, we get it—we're monsters!" yelled Willy "Wi-Fi" Reston from his bunk. "But can you keep it down? I'm trying to tell Nelson he doesn't know anything about video games."

"And I'm trying to tell you you're right!" Nelson shouted back.

"Excuse me?" Mack asked, suddenly interested. "Don't you have a gaming YouTube channel with a million subscribers? And wouldn't that mean you'd have to know a little about the subject?"

The star YouTuber and most famous kid in camp shook his head. "Wi-Fi's right. I'm clueless on the topic."

Mack cocked an eyebrow, waiting for the punch line.

Realizing there was no way out of offering an explanation, Nelson sighed and pulled something from under his pillow. It was a smooth black ball emblazoned with a black number eight in a white circle.

"The Magic 8 Ball?!" Mack moaned, recognizing the item that had become Nelson's totem that summer. "You're still letting that thing make all your choices for you?"

Nelson rolled the toy in his hands. "I wasn't having any luck winning the argument, so when I was in the bathroom, I asked the 8 Ball if I should agree with everything Wi-Fi said. It told me, 'You may rely on it.'"

"TRANSLATION!" Mack yelled, seemingly to nobody.

Miles adjusted his glasses, recognizing his cue. "In this context, that essentially means yes. Therefore, the ball 'told' him to agree with Wi-Fi's every argument."

"How did that work out for you?" Mack asked Nelson.

"About as well as arguing with him did," Nelson deadpanned.

"Hey, that's a cheap shot!" Wi-Fi shouted. "Just get rid of the 8 Ball and talk to me already."

Nelson crossed his arms. "I'll do that when you shake hands with a girl."

Wi-Fi turned white. "Point taken," he said. Though he'd made major strides in conquering his fear of girls since the start of camp, actually making physical contact wasn't one of them. "But I still don't see why we can't have a rational conversation. All I said was that *Gill Warriors 3* is the best massively multiplayer online role-playing game of all time."

"You're absolutely right," Nelson agreed. "*Brainscape 2* doesn't even hold a candle to it, despite what I said on the internet."

"Cut it out!" Wi-Fi shouted.

"You got it!"

"Andre!" Wi-Fi called in reinforcements. "Make him stop!"

By this point, Andre had retreated to his coveted center-room top bunk, which he had won in a foot race with Mack at the start of summer. "Sorry, Wi-Fi," he said with a grin, propping himself up on his elbow. "You're on your own."

"Come on, Andre," Mack said. "Jump in and play ref. It's not like you have anything pressing now that baseball season's over."

Andre closed his eyes and flopped onto his back. "Don't remind me, man! I don't even know what I'm *doing* today. I feel like Pat without a practical joke."

Just then, the door shot open and early morning light poured in from outside. Standing in the frame was Pat himself.

"Very funny!" he shouted at the room, and in particular at Mack. "I woke up in my bed and everything was normal. Except my bed was in cabin 11!"

"How did it get there?!" Mack asked innocently.

"And if you were in cabin 11, who's that?" Andre inquired.

All eyes followed Andre's pointer finger to the sleeping form curled up under a blanket in the lower bunk at the back of the room. At exactly that moment, the unidentified camper threw off his covers, swung his feet to the floor, and stretched his arms out wide in a yawn.

"Special K?!" Pat shrieked.

"Morning!" wheezed Kevin Chu, a member of the baseball team and resident of cabin 11. Then he stood and casually walked the length of the cabin and out the door in his pajamas.

Pat watched the door creak closed behind him, then turned back to his cabinmates. "You guys did this! Fess up!"

"We didn't do this!" Mack said, sounding insulted.

"I mean, this is … it's just *so epic*. Something like this would take, what, a couple of weeks of planning?"

"At least," Andre chimed in.

"At least a couple of weeks," Mack continued. "You'd need to talk to the guys in cabin 11. You'd need to wake up early enough to get a bunk bed out one cabin door, down a set of stairs, up another set of stairs, and into another cabin. Then you'd have to do it all over again on the way back."

Hassan approached the bed from which Kevin had just emerged, resting a hand on the wooden frame. "Can one of these bunk beds even fit through a cabin door?" he asked, playing along.

"Hypothetically speaking?" Mack replied.

"Of course."

"They fit just barely."

Andre jumped off his top bunk and raised a finger in the air. "And that wouldn't even be the hard part."

"No?" Mack asked, interested.

"No. See, those beds are anchored to the wall. You'd need to find a screwdriver and take out the screws. If, say, you were a kid at camp and didn't have access to a screwdriver, you'd have to figure out an alternative."

"Like repurposing a broken metal flipper from the kitchen, if it was a flathead you needed," Miles said matter-of-factly.

"Exactly. Then you'd need to remove both beds from the walls before you could move them."

"And one of them would have a sleeping person in it, so you'd have to be gentle and quiet about the moving part," Mack added.

"Obviously," Andre said.

Mack rubbed his chin for a few seconds, then looked Pat in the eye. "Yeah, man, that's a little far-fetched."

"Whatever!" Pat shouted. "I know it was you guys. I also know you did it so you could get at my lucky silver dollar. But joke's on you. I keep it on me *at all times!*"

In past summers, Pat's signature prank had been to tell people he'd lost his precious silver dollar … when he'd never had one in the first place. But then Mack gave him one during last year's baseball tournament to help him out of a hitting slump.

Now the joke had come full circle. Pat had a silver dollar, but he wouldn't let anyone else lay a hand on it.

"Oh, you've got it on you?" Mack needled his friend. "Let's see it."

"Not on your life!" Pat said, flopping down on the bed that may or may not have been his. "You'd probably just lose it."

CHAPTER
3

"I SORT OF JOINED THE TEAM"

Thirty minutes later, the boys of cabin 13 were in line at the mess hall steam table, standing just underneath a framed eight-by-ten picture of last summer's victorious junior-camp baseball team. It was placed so everyone in the room could see it, and it was cleaned and dusted daily.

Nelson had his Magic 8 Ball out once again. During the school year, he had done a video review on it for his unboxing YouTube channel, and he had been carrying it around in his backpack ever since.

"Do I try the breakfast special?" he whispered to the toy, glancing suspiciously at a steaming tray of corned beef hash. Then he turned the 8 Ball upside down, and a blue triangle appeared in a circular window. It read, "My sources say no."

"Can I help you?" the server at the steam table asked, causing Nelson to recoil in horror.

"No! I mean, no, thank you!" he blurted, then bolted for the cereal bar.

When Nelson sat down next to Pat at the cabin 13 table a couple of minutes later, his tray laden with raisin bran and fruit salad, Mack nodded at his backpack. "I think we need to revisit this," he said in a soothing voice.

"Hey," Nelson said, "lots of people carry around Magic 8 Balls because they don't like making decisions."

"Really?" Mack furrowed his brow.

"There's a whole online message board!"

"Are you sure it's not a prank?" Pat asked, stabbing a pineapple chunk from Nelson's bowl. "Creating a message board like that seems right up *my* alley."

Suddenly a tray dropped onto the table between them, and a girl squeezed onto the edge of Nelson's chair.

"Yes, he's sure!" said Nelson's ten-year-old sister, Cassie. "He checked the individual IP addresses of the other posters."

"Cassie?! I told you about this—you're supposed to sit with your own cabin!"

She waved a hand in his face. "They know where I am." Then she turned to her table and shouted, "Hi, cabin!"

"Hi, Cassie!" her cabinmates and counselors yelled in return.

Cassie was a toy tester like her brother, but unlike him, she was as confident in person as she was onscreen.

"I can't stay long, dudes. I've got ball hockey in a few minutes, and they wouldn't even be able to *find* the net without me. What are you doing today, bro?" she asked, throwing an arm around his waist.

Nelson wriggled out of her embrace. "Thanks a lot, Cass," he said sarcastically. "I was hoping that wouldn't come up."

"What?" Andre asked, a puzzled look on his face.

Nelson sighed loudly. "The 8 Ball told me to join the basketball team."

Mack did a double take. "But you just got your freedom back! Do you even know how to play basketball?"

Cassie scoffed on her brother's behalf. "Our dad grew up in the Philippines, where basketball is *huge*. He nearly played pro before he moved here, and he had us shooting and dribbling before we could walk."

"Then why do you look so nervous?" Andre asked Nelson, studying his face.

"I guess I can shoot a bit," he said, "but I've never *played*. It's two different things."

"Not even in gym class?" Wi-Fi asked.

"We're homeschooled."

"Not even three-on-three?"

"No."

"One-on-one?" Wi-Fi pressed.

"Does the hoop count as 'one'?"

Mack crossed his arms. "This is all interesting, man, but the point stands—you just got out of constant baseball practice, and now you're jumping into constant basketball practice! This confirms it: that 8 Ball is evil!" He turned to Pat and Andre. "At least *you two* made the right call."

Pat beamed, then stood and shouted, "They may take our New Money, but they will never take ... our freedom!"

Though few campers knew what Pat meant or why he was using a Scottish accent, most stood and cheered at the general sentiment. In the pandemonium, no one noticed as Andre simply flushed and rubbed the back of his head.

After breakfast, Mack ran back to cabin 13, grabbed his swimming gear, and headed for the waterfront, a towel slung over his shoulder. As he neared the camp office, Laker rushed out from behind a bush and intercepted him.

"Whoa! Hey, man," Mack's former cabin counselor and baseball coach stammered. "Funny running into you here! What are the odds?"

"I walk this way every day after breakfast," Mack said in a flat tone.

Laker laughed madly, doubling over and slapping his knee. "Good one, Mack. Hey, speaking of ... *that*, it seems there's still a couple of empty spots on the boys' basketball team. Would you have any interest in joining?"

Mack watched with a strange sense of déjà vu as the baseball director squirmed. He could sense that Laker was up to something—or maybe had been *put up* to something—but he didn't want to know what it was.

"Thanks, Laker," he said, "but no thanks."

"But if you do join the team, then I can offer—"

"There's nothing you can say to sweeten the deal," Mack said forcefully. "Outside of *this conversation*, my summer is perfect as it is."

Laker threw up his hands. "Okay, okay, I get it! Just don't say I didn't try."

Mack didn't understand what he meant, but he spun away ... only to run directly into Wi-Fi, Nelson, and a handful of other basketball players.

"Hey ... guys?" he said, noticing Andre among them.

"Hey, Mack," Andre said sheepishly. "I sort of joined the team."

"What?! Since when?"

"Since, like, five minutes ago. So ... wanna shoot some hoops?"

Mack recoiled. "Not you, too, man!"

"Me too, what? I thought you liked basketball! According to last year's athletic testing, you're the best player in junior camp."

"I *do* like basketball! It's my favorite sport. I just don't want to play on the team!"

"Well, nobody's trying to force you!"

"Laker did two minutes ago!"

"Why are we yelling?!"

Mack opened his mouth to shout something else but quickly closed it again. He didn't want to sign up, but what was the harm in Andre's joining?

"We're yelling … because I'm being stupid about this!" Mack shouted.

Andre smiled. "Yeah, you are!"

Both boys giggled, officially defusing the situation.

"Seriously," Mack said, "good luck with the team. Just don't ask me to join."

"After this display?" Andre replied. "Don't worry about it. We don't need any hotheads."

The two engaged in their signature Camp Average handshake—a high five followed by a full-body shrug—and then Andre and the others continued on their way to the field house for practice. Mack turned again toward the waterfront, but he heard his name once more.

"Hey, Mack! Wait up!"

"For the love of water sports!" Mack wailed. "Can I *please* just go swimming?!"

He spun around to find the source of the voice: Miles. He was holding a large rocket and staring at the ground with sad eyes.

"Sorry, man. I didn't know it was you," Mack said guiltily. "What's up?"

Miles beamed. "Wanna watch a rocket launch?"

Mack shot a quick glance at the beach, then back at his friend. "You know it."

CHAPTER 4

"THERE'S A PROBLEM!"

"Ready, Nicole?" asked Brian, the cabin 13 counselor and junior-camp boys' basketball coach.

Nicole nodded, resting her hand on a basketball in a rack to her side and eyeing up a corner three-pointer. She had signed up for the competitive hoops stream along with Makayla and their friend Elena Armstrong, who were both sitting near center court.

"Okay," yelled the girls' coach, Tamara, in a booming voice that demanded attention. She wore a navy-blue tracksuit, and her straight black hair was pulled back into a tight bun. "GO!"

Nicole grabbed the first ball and brought it up beside her head, cradling it in her right hand and guiding it with her left. Putting her legs into the shot, she flicked her right wrist and sent the ball on a high arc toward the hoop. It dropped through the net with a swish.

Then she sank the next four on the rack as well.

"Keep it up!" Tamara shouted as Nicole sprinted to a second rack. "Twenty more shots to go."

Nelson and Wi-Fi hooted their encouragement along with the other kids in the gym, though Wi-Fi was simultaneously edging away from the nearest girl for fear of accidental contact. Andre, meanwhile, looked both impressed and worried. He held the current top score in the three-point competition, but even he hadn't sunk a whole rack during his turn.

Nicole's perfect start gave her a great chance of taking the crown. But as she raised the first ball of the second rack, the room was filled with an ear-splitting screech. Her shot flew over the glass backboard and slammed into the metal supports connecting it to the ceiling.

Members of both teams spun to locate the source of the noise. Their eyes found their camp director, standing just inside the door with a megaphone to his mouth.

"And people tell me I should get this thing fixed!" Winston said into the megaphone, his voice echoing off the walls. "Why would I when I get this kind of attention?!"

The kids and coaches stared at him blankly. After an uncomfortably quiet moment, he raised the megaphone again.

"For the record, that was a rhetorical question," he said. "But I still would have liked some kind of response."

No one budged. The silence stretched past the ten-second mark and lasted until Wi-Fi's allergies kicked in, and he sneezed hard three times.

"Good enough!" Winston said. "Now where was I?"

He walked over to the basket. Nicole looked at Tamara—who shrugged her shoulders in confusion—and then sat down with her teammates.

"I came here today because I'd like to personally thank you all for joining the basketball teams. I'm sure it'll be a great season of competitive activity," Winston said. "And to offer a little reward for all the hard work I know you'll be doing, I've decided to enter us … in a tournament."

Finally, Winston got a reaction as his audience immediately began to chatter and cheer.

"Yes!" Andre pumped his fist.

"A tournament?!" Nicole gasped. "Who with?"

"I hope it's not those jerks from Killington," Wi-Fi said. "I don't think I could handle that."

Winston smiled down on the excited players. "No, Wi-Fi, I don't believe Killington has added basketball to its summer offerings. But there will certainly be some stiff competition."

Then he held up the piece of orange paper in his hand. "We'll be playing in the Swish City 5-on-5."

More gasps. The Swish City 5-on-5 was legendary for the

big names who'd taken part over the years. It had individual brackets for all age groups, and it took place at the end of the summer as a kind of super championship for all the teams who'd spent the season playing in smaller circuits.

"Awesome," breathed Andre.

Nicole grinned at him, and the two high-fived, setting off a series of fist bumps and celebratory seat-dances.

"There's just one problem," Winston said, but no one could hear him. Then he raised his megaphone. "There's a problem!" he blared.

The kids turned their attention to the camp director once again.

"According to the rules," he said, "only one team can represent each organization."

Nelson shook his head. "What does that mean?"

"It means, Nelson, that we can't send both the boys' and the girls' teams."

"Why not?"

"They want to avoid a situation where a powerhouse organization enters multiple teams and ends up playing itself in the finals," Winston explained. "I mean, imagine if Killington could put more than one team in the all-camp baseball tourney. We'd *never* get to the final!"

Andre shuddered at the thought. But then he looked at the sheer number of kids around him. The boys' team wasn't full yet, but it already boasted nine players. The girls' squad had ten. He knew professional teams dressed only twelve, and they played longer games.

"But," Andre wondered aloud, his eyes falling on Nicole, "if we combine the teams, that means some of us won't get to play."

Nicole sneered at him, taking offence on behalf of her team. "By 'some of us,' you mean some of the girls, right?" she asked. "Ha! If we hold tryouts, most of *you* won't get to go."

"Hey, that's not—" Andre started before Winston cut him off.

"So what's our decision?" he asked. "Does the boys' team want to drop out?"

Andre saw his teammates looking at him, and he realized he'd just been elected captain. "No," he told Winston.

"And I'm guessing the same for the girls' team?"

"No," Nicole said before furrowing her brow. "Er, I mean, yes? Same here? We don't want to drop out!"

"Okay, then," Winston said, as if he'd been waiting for this moment. "We will have a best-of-three series to see which of you gets to go."

Players from both teams shifted anxiously. Then a fired-up Andre broke the silence. "It's on!" he shouted. "May the best team represent Camp Average!"

"Avalon!" Winston shouted, to no avail.

"See you on the court!" Nicole shouted back. "Come on, team. Let's go practice outside."

In seconds, she reached the field house door and threw it open … knocking Mack and Miles onto their butts.

Miles's rocket launch had gone off without a hitch. The rocket itself—an ESTES SLV with an E12-4 engine—had blasted a thousand feet straight up into the sky. But when Mack had spotted Winston's white golf cart parked outside the field house on the way back, he suddenly felt as if his stomach had gone with it.

The two boys had watched the whole episode through a crack in the door.

"Hey, Mack. Hey, Miles," Nicole said absently as she stormed past them, the rest of her team in tow.

As Mack helped his friend up, brushing dust and pine needles off his back, he looked through the open field house door to find Winston staring at him. The camp director had a look on his face Mack didn't recognize.

He was smiling.

Mack kept his mouth shut until lights-out that night, but as soon as Brian and Hassan had left the cabin, he grabbed his flashlight and stood next to Andre, shining it in his face.

"I told you so!" he seethed. "I told you joining the basketball team was a bad idea."

"Uh, no." Andre shielded his eyes. "You said *you* didn't want to join. You just kind of freaked out at me and Nelson. And besides, what's so bad about joining the basketball team? Winston got us into a tournament!"

The beam from Mack's flashlight darted around the darkened room as his Zen-like state from the first three weeks of camp disintegrated completely. "Don't you see? This is *classic* Winston! He's pitting you against the girls on purpose, making you fight among yourselves to push you into doing things his way, just like he did last summer."

"I don't know, Mack," Wi-Fi chimed in. "I'm not happy about fighting with Nicole, but that sounds pretty Machiavellian."

"ENCYCLOPEDIA!" Mack whisper-shouted.

"It means 'underhanded,'" Miles said from across the room. "Named after Niccolò Machiavelli, a sixteenth-century Italian politician. He literally wrote the book on devious political behavior."

"Then this is *very* Machiavellian!" Mack seethed. "Winston is Machiavellian to the max-iavellian!"

"Maybe you just need to give him a break," Andre said flatly. He rolled over to face the wall, putting a not-so-subtle end to the conversation.

31

Mack angrily clicked off the flashlight and flopped back into his bed. "Whatever," he fumed. "I just don't want to find out what he has planned next."

CHAPTER 5

"BUT I HAVEN'T DONE ANYTHING THIS TIME"

The next morning, Mack did his best to put Winston out of his mind. He played soccey with Spike and Mike in the cabin, got yelled at for a slap shot that knocked Brian's smartphone to the floor, and held his hands over his ears when Andre and Wi-Fi talked basketball strategy in the mess hall.

As soon as breakfast was done, he made a beeline for the waterfront. He'd already put on swim shorts and wrapped a towel around his neck before leaving the cabin, and there was no need to return there or talk to anyone—so he didn't.

Until he got to his destination.

"Hold up!" yelled Jama, the lifeguard on duty, as Mack sprinted past him toward the dock, yanking off his shoes as he went.

"Why?" Mack asked, skidding to a stop. "Isn't this free swim?"

"Do you see anyone swimming?"

Mack hadn't noticed as he was running up, but the beach was empty. The lake was still, and all canoes, kayaks, and paddleboards were lined up neatly on the shore.

He turned back to Jama. "Is this a prank?" Then he shouted to no one in particular, "Pat, if this is your doing, you are *so* going down."

"It's not a prank, Mack," Jama said. "The waterfront is closed."

"I KNOW WHERE YOU SLEEP, PAT!" Mack yowled.

"Keep your voice down!" Jama pleaded. "Pat had nothing to do with this. There's apparently some sort of microbial pest in the water. They have to conduct some tests to make sure it's safe."

"How long will that take?"

Jama paused. "Could be a couple of weeks," he said. "Or it could be the rest of the summer."

Mack's jaw dropped. He gazed longingly at the beach—so close, yet so far away—and then he gazed beyond it, to Camp Clearwater, the girls' camp across the lake. Though it was a long way off, he could clearly see kids swimming, kids splashing, kids canoeing.

"Why don't they have to shut down their beach?"

Jama looked across the water. "That's funny—I hadn't

thought about it. Maybe it's about currents or some-thing."

"In a lake this small?!"

Jama's eyes narrowed. "Don't look at me. I'm just the messenger. The waterfront is off limits. And *that's that.*"

Mack stared down the lifeguard for an uncomfortable few seconds, then left the beach and marched up the hill to the next best thing: the camp pool. He jumped in on an advanced swim class and spent the rest of the morning honing his butterfly stroke.

He had almost managed to put the beach closure out of his mind when he arrived back at the pool after lunch—and found it drained.

"What is going on?" Mack whispered despondently.

Hassan, who was spending half his day as a swim coach now that baseball season was over, walked up and put a hand on his shoulder.

"It's the weirdest thing—I just found out, too. Apparently, there was a slow leak in the pool, and it was going to start flooding the nearby fields, maybe even mess with some buried wires and electrical stuff."

"But, Hassan, I was *just in the pool*. I didn't notice any slow leaks."

"That's why it's called a *slow* leak, man. It's so slow you can't even see it."

"So when can we start using it again?" Mack said weakly. "Later this afternoon or … ?"

"No such luck, I'm afraid. It needs a major patch job, and pool-maintenance people aren't easy to come by in the middle of summer. Could be a while."

Mack studied Hassan's face. The previous summer, the two had seen eye to eye on Winston's underhanded tactics, but the older boy hadn't exactly supported Mack's schemes, either. Now he couldn't be sure whose side Hassan was on.

"So you see nothing out of the ordinary here?" Mack asked the counselor, watching his expression closely. "The beach and the pool, my two favorite places at camp, get shut down hours apart. That doesn't seem weird to you?"

Hassan chuckled. "No, I don't see anything out of the ordinary, Mack. And to answer your real question—no, I don't think Winston bored a hole in the pool."

"But—"

Hassan held up both hands in a stopping motion. "Lake water gets gross, and pools get leaks. It's a major bummer, and I feel for you, but that doesn't mean it's a conspiracy."

Mack disagreed, and over the next two days, he got loads more evidence for his case.

The morning after the pool closure, Mack signed up for archery. But when he got to the range, he found that ants had infested it.

He chose the ropes course, but counselors there told him a bald eagle had turned the site into a nesting ground.

Orienteering? A sudden but complete compass shortage meant they had to shut down until they could get more.

By that point, Mack had realized that arguing with the counselors would do no good. But as he turned away from yet another noncompetitive activity, he noticed a large group of frustrated campers standing nearby ... and felt guilty by force of habit. The summer before, he'd made a lot of decisions that led to an escalating series of punishments, from earlier wake-up times to a grueling boot camp. And none of his fellow campers had been happy about any of it.

But I haven't done anything this time, Mack thought as he walked off.

In his heart, though, he knew that was the problem: he felt sure that Winston had orchestrated all this because he wanted Mack to get off the sidelines and do *something*. And Mack was certain he knew what that something was.

CHAPTER
6

"REPLY HAZY, TRY AGAIN"

After lights-out that night, Mack lay on his bed, training his flashlight on a camp brochure. "So my options are down to competitive sports … or rocketry," he said miserably.

"Sounds like an easy call to me!" Miles said, putting down a book called *Model Rockets for Model Citizens*.

"If these accidents keep happening, they're going to have to think up a new name for this place," mused Pat. "Camp Inaccessible? Camp All-Out-of-Luck?"

Mack took a deep breath. "I don't know, Pat," he began slowly. "I'm starting to think luck has nothing to do with this."

"What do you mean?" Miles asked.

"For starters, I don't think the lake should be inaccessible at all."

"Wait—you *want* to get whatever super swimmer's itch is waiting for you at our beach?" Andre asked from his bunk above Mack's.

"No, I'm saying what if there is no swimmer's itch at all?"

Wi-Fi pointed his flashlight at his own face. "Oh, swimmer's itch is all too real," he said. "My cousin got it once, and her skin crawled for days!"

"I know swimmer's itch is real! I just—"

"She can't even look at lake water now," Wi-Fi continued.

Mack couldn't take anymore. "I just think Winston is behind this!"

His cabinmates groaned.

"You think Winston *poisoned the lake*?!" Andre said. "It's not like he's Pat!"

Pat thumped the wall in protest. "You *accidentally* poison a baseball team one time and you get branded for life."

"No, I don't think he … well, I don't want to rule anything out," Mack said. "But mainly I think he just made the whole thing up."

"Why would he do that?" Nelson asked sincerely.

Mack paused, then mumble-whispered something his cabinmates couldn't hear.

"What?" they asked in unison.

"He wants me to play on the basketball team," Mack blurted.

The boys sat silent for a few moments, then they all burst out laughing.

"Winston poisoned a lake to get you to play basketball?" Pat howled mockingly, drawing a shush from the counselor on duty outside their cabin. "That is the craziest thing I've ever heard, and I mean, I currently have a silver dollar duct-taped to a part of my body I will never reveal to you guys!"

Andre wiped tears of laughter off his cheeks with his T-shirt, then hung upside down from his bunk to talk to Mack face-to-face. "So let's say for a second that you're right," he began. "How do you know he's not trying to get you to play competitive ball hockey? Or, like, golf?"

"I'm not good at ball hockey. I'm not good at golf. And besides, the basketball tournament is the biggest thing left on the schedule this summer."

Andre snorted. "I hate to break it to you, man, but he doesn't need this tournament that badly, and you're not *that* good at basketball. *Nobody's* that good."

Wi-Fi put a hand to his chin. "You know, Steph Curry might be that good."

"He's great," Andre answered. "But is he poisoning-a-lake-to-get-him-to-play-for-you great?"

"How big is the lake?" Wi-Fi asked. "And does my cousin have to swim in it?"

As Andre contemplated this, Mack yanked at his head of messy brown hair, defeated.

"We're all sorry about the beach and pool closing, Mack," Miles said soothingly. "Seriously, though, rocketry is fun. I can show you the ropes while the other things get sorted out."

But with each passing moment, Mack was more and more sure that taking Miles's offer wasn't an option—that if he joined rocketry, Winston would shut it down just as he had everything else.

And from there, he saw the rest of the summer unfold like a bad dream. If rocketry disappeared and Mack chose, say, competitive tennis, Winston would fake a localized earthquake to break up the cement court. If he picked soccer, Winston would flood the field. (He could even claim the pool leak had something to do with it.)

How far would he go, and how long was Mack willing to hold out?

Mack had his principles, but were they more valuable than every other camper's good time?

The next morning, Mack was still wrestling with his decision. As everyone filed out of the cabin, a hand grabbed his shoulder. He turned to find Nelson standing behind him.

"Just wanted to say, I believe you about Winston."

Mack felt a wave of gratitude wash over him, but he couldn't help asking why.

"Well, you weren't wrong last time," Nelson said. "Plus, you've been at this camp forever. If you think something's up, then you're probably on to something."

"Thanks," Mack said, holding out his fist for Nelson to dap. "But that doesn't fix my main problem."

"Which is?"

"If I'm right—if *we're* right—and Winston's willing to do *anything* to get me on that basketball team, then I need to join or we're all going to suffer. And I had enough of that feeling last summer—being the guy whose decisions hurt others."

"But … ?"

"But I don't want to give him what he wants. I don't want him to win. Again."

Nelson whistled through his teeth. "Sounds like one for the Magic 8 Ball," he said jokingly.

Mack's eyes went wide. "That's it!"

"What's it?"

"The Magic 8 Ball! I can't make this decision, so I'll leave it up to fate!"

"Oh no," Nelson said. "No, that's not a good idea. It's one thing for me to let it choose my dinner options. It's not supposed to decide the destiny of the *entire* camp."

Nelson tried to sneak around Mack to the door, but his friend blocked his path.

"Come on, man," he pleaded. "You gotta help me. I'm out of options."

Nelson realized he was, too. He pulled the Magic 8 Ball out of his backpack and handed it over.

"Should I join the basketball team?" Mack asked. Then he turned the ball over and watched as the blue triangle rose to the top.

"Reply hazy, try again," it read.

He repeated the process.

"Ask again later," the toy advised.

"What do you mean, 'later'?" Mack shouted. "I don't have time to wait for 'later'!"

"Calm down, man," Nelson said nervously.

Mack asked his question a third time.

"Better not tell you now," the 8 Ball offered.

"What is going on with this thing?" Mack shook the toy wildly up and down. "Should I join the basketball team or not?"

"Stop it, man!" Nelson said. "You're filling it with air bubbles!" He abruptly reached out to grab the ball, but Mack yanked it away.

Then he lost his grip.

The 8 Ball flew out of his hand, and he spun to watch it trace an arc through the air as it sailed toward the back of the cabin.

"NOOOOOOOOO!" the boys shouted, but there was no stopping the ball's momentum. It landed hard on the floor and cracked in half, shooting blue dye in all directions—on the blankets and furniture legs and storage bins at the back of the room.

The ball came to rest in a puddle of blue liquid, and Nelson slumped to the ground.

"Oh, man. I'm so sorry," Mack said. "I didn't want that to happen."

Neither of them moved. Then Nelson replied, "It's okay."

"No," Mack insisted. "It really isn't."

"Actually," Nelson said a little louder, "it's kind of a relief." He took a few breaths. "I needed to break up with that thing but didn't know how. Straight-up breaking it does the trick."

Mack smiled weakly and put a hand on his friend's shoulder. "Well, at least let me do the cleanup."

He stooped to pick up the pieces of the broken toy and realized he still didn't have an answer to his question: Should he play basketball?

Then, underneath a large piece of black plastic, he found a white twenty-sided die sitting in a pool of blue goo.

He read the side facing him: "It is decidedly so."

CHAPTER
7

"LOOK WHO CAME CRAWLING BACK"

"I've come to join the basketball team!"

Mack was dressed in a sleeveless white T-shirt, blue shorts, and black high-tops, but he entered the camp office and made his pronouncement like the messenger of a foreign power. Only there was no large welcoming party inside—just Cheryl, the camp's longtime facilities administrator.

"I can see that," she said, before bringing Mack's schedule up on her laptop and quickly hitting a few keys.

"And ... done. You're all set up."

Mack frowned. He'd agonized over the decision and had finally opted to put the good of the camp ahead of his vendetta against Winston—with a little help from the Magic 8 Ball. But the end result of that painful process felt a lot like ... signing up for a basketball team.

"That's it?" he asked.

"That's it," Cheryl replied cheerfully as she brought

up the program guide. "The boys' team is just starting practice now in the field house, so if you hurry, you can join them."

Mack hesitated, then decided to try a strategy he'd picked up watching TV courtroom dramas with his grandma: leading the witness. "I bet Winston will be happy."

"Oh, yeah?" Cheryl said, focused on a newly arrived email.

"Yeah. I heard he really wants me to—I mean, he wants more players for the team," Mack offered.

"He does love to cheer you guys on," Cheryl said absently.

The phone rang, and she picked it up.

"Camp Avalon … can you hold, please?" She put her hand over the receiver. "Anything else, Mack?"

Mack could see he was getting nowhere. "No, uh, thanks for the help," he said and ducked out the door.

"Well, look who came crawling back," Andre said, stopping the basketball team's stretching routine as Mack walked into the gym.

Mack offered a cocky grin. "Yeah, well, I saw who was on the team and figured I couldn't just let you guys get run off the floor."

"Boo! Hiss!" yelled Wi-Fi as others joined in the gleeful jeering.

"Welcome to the team, Mack," Brian said. "Glad you changed your mind. The girls' team is going to be tough, and we can use your help."

Mack's face went red, but he hid it behind his arm as he joined the group for stretches. Joining the team? Yes. Helping the team? Not part of the plan. He would show up for practices and games, but he had no interest in killing himself for a team he didn't care about. And he figured that would be enough. The big tournament was set for the last weekend of camp, so even if the boys' team made it there and didn't win a game, it'd be too late for Winston to punish anyone for it—something he'd been known to do in the past.

"All right, guys, bring it in," Brian said when the warm-up was done.

The ten players knelt in a semicircle around their coach.

"So Mack already knows Andre, Wi-Fi, and Nelson. The rest of you, stand and introduce yourselves."

First up was a skinny boy with dark skin and short curly dark hair. He was easily two inches shorter than everyone else in the gym. "I'm Elijah Carter. I play point guard—until I hit my growth spurt. Then I'm going to live in the paint and dunk everything."

Elijah fist-bumped his nearby teammates, and Brian moved on to the next boy in the row: Gavin Gates. He had red hair and freckles, and was slathered in sunscreen even in the field house.

"I'll do whatever," he said, "but I think of myself as a shooting guard."

Next: an athletic-looking boy named Omar Khoury who said he was more of a defender than a shooter.

"So like a *guarding* guard, maybe?" he joked.

And finally, a trio of long-armed forwards: Luis Rodriguez, Darnell Cruse, and Dillon Woods. Mack couldn't remember ever seeing Dillon before, but he suddenly wondered how that was possible: the gangly, scraggly haired twelve-year-old wore a scowl on his face and a camp T-shirt cut down the front to look like he'd been slashed by a werewolf.

Roll call out of the way, Brian set about running practice. Mack was instantly impressed. "Okay," the coach announced, "let's run a three-man weave. I need three separate lines on the baseline: one on each sideline and one under the basket."

Mack lined up behind Wi-Fi in the middle of the court and watched as a nervous-looking Nelson followed Andre to the left sideline.

"Just watch me," Andre reassured him. "You'll pick it up."

Brian tossed a ball to Wi-Fi, who patted it to start the drill. Both Andre on his left and Gavin on his right started running at a forty-five-degree angle toward the center of the court. Wi-Fi expertly flicked the ball to Andre and followed his own pass, circling around him. Then Andre hit Gavin with a sharp pass of his own and circled around him in the same way.

"Good!" Brian shouted. "Don't let the ball hit the floor!"

The three carefully jogged up the court, snapping passes and filling in lanes until Wi-Fi sent a shovel pass—a quick underhand toss—to Andre, who banked a left-handed layup into the hoop.

As the three weaved their way back toward the rest of the team, Mack looked over at Nelson. He was slowly turning green, as if their every step drew him closer to his own demise.

Wi-Fi finished the drill with a short jump shot that flitted through the nylon mesh into Mack's waiting arms.

"Okay, next group!" Brian yelled. "First pass to the right wing this time."

Luis raced off the baseline. Mack hit him with a text-book chest pass, flicking his wrists to create backspin, and a split second later, the ball had been flipped on to Nelson.

But as Mack circled around Luis and got ready for a pass, Nelson froze up, running with the ball instead of letting it go.

Mack raised his hands to chest height to make a target, and Nelson's eyes grew wide with recognition. He pulled the ball into his stomach and pushed it back outward with all his might … right into Mack's left cheek.

"Oooooh!" a few players said. Others grimaced as Mack hit the ground, clutching his face.

"I'm sorry, Mack!" Nelson blurted, flopping onto the floor next to him. The rest of the team ran up and huddled around them. "I panicked! Are you okay?"

Brian raced to the first-aid kit on the sideline, grabbed a small white plastic bag, and pushed to the center of the group. "Give him some room, guys."

Mack pulled a hand away from his cheek to accept the ice pack, revealing a large red welt that was sure to turn into a black eye.

"Ooooooooooh," a few of his teammates said again.

"Mack!" Nelson wailed. "Can you see me?!"

"It's okay, New Money," Mack said. "I'm going to live."

"Forgive me!" Nelson said.

Mack winced as he planted the freezing-cold bag on his cheek. "Let's just say this makes us even for the 8 Ball."

Nelson beamed. "Done!"

His face throbbing from the ball and freezing from the ice pack, Mack took a seat on the sideline as the team ran through the drill several more times, somehow getting sloppier as they went.

"Talk!" Brian shouted. "Communicate! Say the name of the guy you're passing to!"

The players on the court shot confused looks at each other—why name the guy when he's the only passing option?—but followed the coach's order anyway.

"Andre!"

"Gavin!"

"Wi-Fi!"

Hearing their names helped the players focus, and Mack saw the passes get crisper and the weave tighter until his teammates looked more like volleyball players tapping the ball to each other.

After the three-man weave, Mack left the ice pack on the sideline and returned to the court for a refresher on setting screens—making a one-person wall to block the movement of a teammate's defender. Mack was standing in Omar's way so Andre could dribble freely toward the hoop when Cheryl's voice came over the crackly camp loudspeaker.

"Good news, campers! The waterfront has been declared free from all harmful microscopic parasites and will be back open after lunch."

The boys in the field house cheered, but not so loudly that they couldn't hear the shouts of approval coming from all over camp.

"Also, the pool is back open," Cheryl continued. "And so is the archery range. And the ropes course, the camp radio station ..."

As his teammates high-fived, Mack smiled to himself. Though he wasn't going to say it out loud, he knew those activities didn't just happen to open as soon as he'd joined the basketball team. He was more convinced than ever that Winston was up to something, but he was also sure he'd figured out how to keep him from ruining everyone else's summer.

"... and the horseshoe pit," Cheryl concluded, nearly out of breath. "Have a great day!"

"Believe me," Mack mumbled, "I'm trying."

A few minutes later, Brian set up by the field house door to high-five his players as they left for the mess hall for lunch.

"We'll see you tomorrow for morning practice, right?" he asked when Mack passed by, knowing full well the team's newest member would be spending the afternoon at the waterfront.

"You know it," Mack answered.

Despite knowing deep in his heart that he had no

choice in the matter, he couldn't help but feel slightly—just slightly—okay with it. Basketball *was* his favorite sport, after all, and three of his best friends were on the team.

Maybe, he thought, *this won't be so bad after all.*

CHAPTER
8

"WHAT DIRTY TRICKS?"

By the time Mack got to the waterfront after lunch, he felt lighter than air. Two girls and a boy were already waiting on the dock, life jackets clipped tight, as Jama drifted up in a speedboat. Another counselor grabbed the boat's towline and pulled it in close, and the three kids climbed in.

"Hurry up, Mack!" Jama yelled from the driver's seat. "And don't forget a jacket!"

A grinning Mack ducked into the lifeguard station's equipment room, a narrow shed-like space packed with everything needed for a summer at the beach, from oars to water skis to kayaking helmets. Its walls were lined with red-and-blue life jackets in all sizes, and Mack reached for a medium. But he didn't get the chance to pull it down.

"Psst!"

Mack jumped a full inch off the ground, and the hairs

on the back of his neck stood on end. His first thought: *Please don't let this snake be poisonous!*

Then he heard it again.

"PSSSSSST! OVER HERE!"

Unless snakes—poisonous or otherwise—had learned to talk, Mack was in the clear. He turned in place, quickly scanning every square inch of the tiny shed, but saw no one. Then he noticed a small hole in the wall—and an eyeball staring at him.

"Hey! It's me!"

Mack immediately recognized the voice of his old counselor and baseball coach. He had apparently found a way to squeeze himself into the space between the equipment room and the rest of the lifeguard station.

"Laker? What are you doing?"

"Shh! Keep your voice down. I have to talk to—"

A shout from the beach cut him off.

"Mack!" Jama yelled. "You skiing or not?"

Mack looked out the door, then back at the pleading eye peering through the hole.

He sighed hard, then poked his head out of the shed.

"I'll get the next one!" he shouted. "It's just … taking me a while to pick a life jacket!"

Mack's pronouncement drew five blank stares. Then Jama shrugged his shoulders, waited for his fellow counselor to jump in the boat, and hit the throttle. Within moments the first skier was up on her feet, spraying water left and right, and basically having the time of Mack's life.

Mack retreated into the darkened shed, and Laker immediately started talking, his voice muffled behind the thin wood. "As I was saying, I need to tell you something, but ... what happened to your face?!"

Mack reached up and touched the swollen area under his eye, sending a sharp burst of pain through his head.

"Nothing," he said angrily. "Besides, I get to ask the questions. First things first: How long have you been standing there?"

"I don't know exactly. A while."

"Why don't you come out?"

"Because I can't be seen! And, you know, I haven't figured out how I'm going to do it yet." Laker shifted awkwardly within the wall. "But that's not important right now. What's important is, you can't win the Swish City tournament."

Mack had a sudden vision of himself out on the water, kicking off a ski and holding the towrope in one hand. Water was flicking off his hair, and his eyes were wide open in excitement and happiness. He had given up that ... for *this*?

"Laker, what are you even talking about?! If you wanted to rag on the basketball team, you could have done it at the mess hall."

"That's not what I'm saying!"

"And besides, usually I'd agree with you, but that team is actually pretty good."

"No, I mean: You *can't* win it. You shouldn't *try* to win it. Because if you do"—Laker paused dramatically—"then Winston wins, too."

That got Mack's attention. Obviously, the camp director vastly preferred winning to losing. He reminded them of that fact every day. But Mack could sense that Laker meant something else. His voice went icily cold. "How so?"

"Everyone thought the baseball tournament last summer was just the beginning—that the competitive stream meant we'd need to immediately build a bigger trophy case. Or, you know, *a* trophy case," Laker said. "But you guys just keep losing."

Mack rolled his eyes. "Thanks a lot. I'll tell Andre you send your regards."

"I didn't mean it like that!"

Mack was unmoved. "Remind me to come to your … um, whatever it is you like doing in your spare time, stop you from doing it, and then insult your friends."

Laker's head touched the wall between them with

a quiet thud. "I don't doubt that our basketball teams are good," he pressed on wearily. "That's why I'm here. See, when the board agreed to hire Winston, he didn't promise only one win. He promised *wins*, plural."

"Wait!" Mack said. "Board? What board?"

"The board of directors," Laker said. "Who did you think hired him?"

Mack realized he'd never thought about it. Really, who would hire a guy like Winston to look after a bunch of kids?

"Well, who are they?" he asked, picturing a boardroom full of solemn people in short shorts and knee-high socks.

"I have no idea. I'm not that important," Laker replied. "But the point is this: the Swish City tournament is Camp Avalon's—"

"Camp Average's," Mack corrected.

"Camp Average's last chance this summer for Winston to hold up his end of the bargain. If we win it, he has kept his promise and gets to stay. If we lose … he's gone."

Mack whistled. Just thinking about Winston's little golf cart speeding up the hill and out of camp forever gave him the warm and fuzzies.

But then something else occurred to him. "Why are you telling me this now?" he asked. "A few days ago, you were trying to sign me up for the basketball team."

Laker let out a long breath. "I don't know. Even last

year, I didn't like how he treated you guys, but I was caught in the middle. I wanted to keep my job and tried to make the best of it."

There was a pain in Laker's voice as he spoke, and Mack was reminded of how the baseball coach had been required to carry out all of Winston's orders—running monotonous all-day practices, taking away privileges, instituting boot camp.

"But now," Laker said with a sigh, "maybe I'm just tired of him getting rewarded for his dirty tricks."

Again, he managed to draw Mack's laser focus. "What dirty tricks? Specifically speaking."

Laker shut his one visible eye tightly. "Like starting a fight between the boys' and girls' basketball teams to get them to work harder. And … closing the waterfront to coax you into joining the boys."

"I KNEW it!" Mack half-shouted. "Nobody believed me except Nelson, but I knew it the whole time!"

"I swear, he didn't involve me in this one," Laker said. "He didn't involve anyone. I only found out after noticing the pattern … but then it was plain as day."

Mack snorted regretfully. "You'd think so, wouldn't you?"

"But his plan makes sense, in a sick kind of way," Laker continued. "He wanted to send the best team possible to that tournament, and that meant recruiting you by whatever means necessary. Either you'd make the boys good enough to beat the girls and represent Camp Avalon—"

"Camp Average."

"Or the girls would figure out how to beat you and become better in the process."

"'Pressure makes plastic trophies,'" Mack said, quoting one of Winston's favorite sayings.

"Yeah," Laker grunted. "But he went way too far. When I realized what was going on, I had to say something."

Mack's chest puffed out in vindication. "So how are you going to stop him?"

"*This* is what I'm doing," Laker said quickly. "I don't have any control over the basketball teams. And if I speak out, Winston will just deny everything and send me packing."

"So … ?" Mack said, scratching his head.

"So it's up to you now."

Mack's eyes ballooned. "Me?! Why me?"

Laker laughed. "Why *you*? I mean, why is it always you? Last summer, nearly every kid in camp had a problem with Winston. Only you organized a covert uprising against him."

"But that was last summer," Mack whined. "There has to be someone else."

Laker barreled through. "You think that Batman just gets to hope someone else stops the Joker?"

"Oh, great, so I'm Batman now?!"

Laker was quiet for a few seconds. "Aquaman, then?"

Mack made an involuntary "Pfft!" sound, spraying spittle all over the wall between them.

"Honestly," Laker continued, "do you have another idea about who could do this? You want me to ask Andre?"

Mack let out a long, slow breath. No, he didn't want him to ask Andre. He wanted his friend as far away from this as possible. And with that, he was out of arguments. Winston had to be stopped, and Mack had to be the one to do it. It wasn't enough not to help his teammates win. He had to actively help them lose.

Again.

"I don't want Andre involved," Mack said. "But I can't do this alone."

Laker pumped his fist—he'd convinced Mack of something for the first time ever—and accidentally punched the wall in the process. "I thought of that," he said with a whimper. "I've got an idea, but ..."

"But what?" Mack asked.

"You're not going to like it."

CHAPTER
9

"FINALLY, SOME ACTION!"

Mack trudged up the hill from cabin 13, each step taking him farther away from the speedboat that would leave without him yet again. It was the day after his talk with Laker, and he'd spent the morning in basketball practice. The swelling on his face had already started going down, leaving behind a large purplish bruise above and below his eye. But now, instead of finally, mercifully going waterskiing, he was headed to the camp's underused craft shop and the first-ever session of advanced rocketry, a program Miles had been requesting ever since he'd arrived at Camp Average four years earlier. On the official list of attendees: Miles, Pat, Nelson, Special K, and Mack himself.

Mack pushed open the door of the craft shop, a wide brown building with a red roof, to reveal a single chaotically decorated room. Shelves full of art supplies dominated all four walls, and the long wooden table at the center of the room was covered in nicks, scratches, and every imaginable color of paint. Old dream catchers and macramé plant hangers, either unfinished or forgotten, dangled from randomly placed rusty nails. The only thing about the place that said "rocketry" was Miles, who was already sitting at the table with the rest of the crew.

Mack had to give Laker credit: his old coach knew him pretty well. He *definitely* didn't like this part of the plan. But he also had to acknowledge that by creating this program and signing them all up for it, Laker had given them a serviceable cover story. Mack and the others could explain away their sudden interest in rockets by pointing to their friendship with Miles, and now the newly assembled team had a perfect opportunity to speak freely.

Except for one thing.

"Uh, New Money?" Mack whispered to Nelson once he'd taken his seat at the table. "What's Cassie doing here?"

Cassie was sitting next to Nelson, her rickety chair crowding his.

"Hey, you want to tell her to leave?" Nelson answered too loudly. "Be my guest."

Cassie thrust herself forward to glare at Mack, who turned red and looked away.

"Nobody should leave! Rocketry is for everyone,"

Miles chimed in. "I just wouldn't have expected so many beginners at an advanced class. Also, I have a few questions. First one: Who's our counselor for this?"

"Laker," Mack answered, trying to avoid looking at Cassie.

"Next one: Does he know anything about rocketry?"

"I don't think so."

"Next one: Where is he?"

"Not here."

"Next one: Where is the rocketry equipment?"

"Miles, I'm getting to that—"

Cassie cut him off. "Next one: Are you guys always this boring?"

"If you want to go, Cassie, there's the door!" Mack pointed.

Pat pounded his fist on the table dramatically, stifling a smile. "I, for one, want her to stay," he said. "She tells it like it is. She's the type of person to say something like, 'This rocketry class makes even less sense than *rocket science.*'"

Cassie nodded. "He's right. I *would* say that."

"What's really going on here, Mack?" Miles asked.

"I've been trying to tell you for the past five minutes! This was never supposed to be a rocketry class, advanced or otherwise. It's a secret meeting."

"Secret what-now?" Special K blinked. "What are we meeting about?"

Mack cleared his throat. "We're meeting about taking down Winston."

Five sets of eyes bugged out.

"WHAT?!" Nelson pushed away from the table in horror.

"And to do it," Mack forged ahead, "we need to sabotage *both* the boys' and the girls' basketball teams. No matter which one ends up going to the Swish City tournament, they can't be in any shape to win."

"NO!" Nelson screamed.

"YES!" his sister said, holding both her fists in the air. "Finally, some *action!*"

Pat grinned. "It's official: I like this kid."

"Why did you include me?" Nelson moaned. "I'm actually *on* the boys' team."

Mack looked him in the eye. "I included you because this is important. But also"—he paused—"because you believed me. When I told everyone I thought Winston was up to no good, you were the only one who didn't laugh in my face."

Nelson turned away from the group. "Should I have just kept my mouth shut?" he asked quietly and flipped the twenty-sided die he'd reclaimed from the wreckage of the 8 Ball. It read, "Signs point to yes," and he nodded gravely.

"I was right all along, by the way, and Laker confirmed it," Mack continued. "Winston *was* behind all the closures. And he deliberately pitted the boys' and girls' teams against each other to force their best out of them—rather than just, you know, encouraging them like a normal person would."

Mack outlined the rest of Winston's plot, and the group was captivated.

"So Winston did all that stuff," Special K asked once Mack was finished, "just for a slightly better chance of winning the Swish City tournament?"

"Exactly. It's dia … diablo …" Mack began to mutter before finally shouting, "DICTIONARY!"

"I think you're reaching for 'diabolical,'" Miles said.

"Diabolical—exactly. He'll do anything, hurt anyone, to get what he wants. And if we let him do it, this place will never be the same. It's … diabolical."

"You said that already," Pat interjected helpfully.

"THESAURUS!" Mack yelled.

Miles counted off the synonyms on his hands. "Fiendish, heinous, ruthless—"

"All those things."

"Unconscionable."

"Thanks, Miles."

"Unscrupulous."

"THANKS, MILES!"

Miles beamed. "You're welcome!"

Special K furrowed his brow. "Okay, we need to stop Winston, and to do that, our basketball teams need to lose the tournament. But how do we make that happen? Go up and ask them to do it? That didn't work out so well last summer."

"No, it didn't," Mack agreed. "And it wouldn't work here. Winston wants me involved because he wants the most experienced players on the floor, but he'll be watching like a hawk for any signs of sabotage." He took a breath. "I know you're all probably wondering why Andre isn't here …"

"Who's Andre?" Cassie asked earnestly.

"And this is precisely why. I don't want anyone on the teams to know what we're doing—"

"Okay, cool. Then I can go!" Nelson said, getting up out of his chair.

"*Except Nelson*, and least of all Andre."

Nelson sat back down, crossing his arms in a huff.

"Losing on purpose might just get us punished again, and it would definitely kill Andre," Mack said quietly. "He loves sports and competing, and that's part of the reason he's good at everything—including basketball. But if we do our job right, he won't know we did anything at all. He'll just think his team came close but didn't win, like the baseball team did. No harm, no foul."

Mack looked at the faces of his potential accomplices as they thought his idea through.

"So what's the plan, then?" Pat asked finally.

Before Mack could speak, Cassie jumped in. "Sounds to me like we could just injure this Andre person—"

"HEY!" her brother shouted.

"We are *not* injuring anyone!" wailed Mack.

"Also," Nelson said, "you totally know who Andre is. Green baseball cap? Sleeps in our cabin? You eat breakfast with him pretty much every morning."

"Oh, the *baseball guy*! Why didn't you say so?!" Cassie said. "But still, it's not like I want to send him to the hospital. Just maybe he slips on the basketball court and bruises his tailbone or something. 'Oh no, poor baseball guy has to miss the tournament. So sad!'"

Pat leaned back in his chair. "Yeah, not even I would do something like that," he told her. "But keep the ideas coming!"

Mack pulled his hand down his face in exasperation, careful to avoid his massive bruise. Then he leaned forward and laid both of his arms on the table, as if capturing his plan between them. "I repeat: We don't need to injure anyone. We just need to keep the basketball teams from getting better."

"And how do we do that?" Miles asked.

Mack's black eye twinkled. They had finally got around to a part of the plan he liked.

"By going undercover," he said.

CHAPTER
10

"WHO SLIPS ON
A BANANA PEEL?"

"We are go for Operation Peel Out," Mack whispered under his breath as he stood in the steam-table lineup the following morning. At the cereal bar a few feet away, Pat delicately peeled a banana, dropped the skin on his tray, and bit off a full three-quarters of the fruit, his cheeks bulging.

"Is this absolutely necessary?" asked Miles, pressed up behind him in line.

"Well, Pat didn't need to shove the banana in his mouth all at once—"

"No, I mean all of it. The whole plan."

"Miles," Mack said, sighing his friend's name, "we've been over this. I can influence the boys' team from the inside, but we still need to get to the girls."

The day before, the group had decided that the best way to hinder improvement was to force both sets of players to learn skills they wouldn't actually need. Mack had racked his brain and finally come up with an idea: zone defense.

In a zone defense, each player guards an area on the court rather than a specific opponent. The team on offense can learn to beat it by figuring out where the gaps are, but that takes practice time—time that would be completely wasted if the other team never intended to play zone defense at all.

"The best way to influence the girls is through Nicole, but that will take someone who knows her," Mack continued. "Which means it's either you or me, and you said you didn't want to do it."

"Absolutely not," Miles huffed. "I want as little to do with this plan as possible."

"Then there you go. Operation Peel Out it is."

"But you could just offer Nicole your help. Tell her you never wanted to play, so you're sabotaging the boys' team. She'd listen to you!"

Mack shook his head. "If I walk up and say, 'Hey, here's all our plays,' she'll know something's up. We need her to feel like I owe her a huge debt, and for that to work, she needs to do something big for me. Like save my life."

"You're not going to risk your life over this!"

"Shh!" Mack said, cupping his hand over his friend's mouth. He looked around at the groggy campers near them in line, but nobody seemed awake enough to have heard anything. "It's a banana peel. I don't even think they're actually slippery. It just needs to look good."

At the cereal bar, Pat choked down the final quarter of his banana. He then added a bowl of corn flakes to his tray and carried it off toward the back corner of the mess hall.

As he passed the designated eating area for cabin 15, Nicole's cabin, he stealthily pulled the banana peel off his tray and dropped it. It splayed perfectly, end pointing up and inner peel down, just a couple of feet from Nicole's side.

"I can't believe it," Miles whispered in line. "He did his part."

"And now it's time for mine," Mack said.

He collected a plate of scrambled eggs, bacon, and multigrain toast, and followed Pat's path to Nicole's table. As he approached, Nicole avoided eye contact. She hadn't said a word to him since he'd joined the boys' team.

From her perspective, Mack guessed, it looked like he'd joined to keep the girls from making the tournament. That was the furthest thing from the truth, but there was no way for her to know that.

Still, for this plan to work, she needed to look at him. He had to think fast. *"Fancy meeting you here"? "Long time no see"? "Nice weather we're having"?* He was only steps away from the banana peel now and time was up.

"Hello … everyone," he said, his voice cracking.

Nicole's head spun toward him, her eyebrows crooked with confusion at the stilted greeting.

Good enough, Mack thought.

He stepped on the peel, ready to fake a slow fall into Nicole's arms, but immediately his right foot shot out from under him, sending the peel hurtling into the distance and leaving him momentarily suspended in midair. A look of surprise and terror crossed his face, and before Nicole could move a muscle, he fell flat on his back. As he lay there, his plate and tray clattered to the floor and the various elements of his breakfast landed on his chest and face: eggs, followed by bacon, followed by toast.

Nicole leapt to his side, brushing food from his brow. "Mack! Are you okay?"

"Who?! What?!" Mack gasped, momentarily stunned.

Nicole presented three fingers to her disoriented friend. "How many fingers am I holding up?"

"We're running a zone defense!" he blurted.

Nicole shook her head and blinked, trying to process what she'd heard. As Mack came to and realized what he'd done, he studied her face. First confusion. Then skepticism. Then … he couldn't be sure, but it looked like joy.

She spun around to her cabinmates, now huddled

around her. "He's delirious!" she told them. "And he just said the boys are running a zone defense!"

Mack started breathing hard and tried to look panicked, playing along. "Just forget I said anything!" he stammered.

Nicole turned back to him. "Forget what?" she said, winking. "I won't mention anything if you don't."

Mack got Nicole's meaning: so long as he didn't tell his teammates they needed to change tactics, she wouldn't embarrass him by mentioning his "slipup." Which, amazingly, worked just fine for his secret mission.

He got to his feet and looked down at his tray, which, of course, was empty.

"Help him out, girls!" Nicole said.

"No, that's—" Mack tried to say, but the members of cabin 15 went right to work scraping bacon and scrambled eggs back onto his plate, and then slamming it down on his tray. It was just as before—only dirtier. He'd momentarily felt bad about both deceiving the girls' team and making a mess on the floor. But now, judging by the amount of sand and dirt dotting his eggs, he realized his fall may have actually helped the janitorial staff. So there was that.

But where was his second piece of toast? "Thanks," he mumbled, too embarrassed to go looking for it.

Mack took a shaky step toward his own table, but he didn't get any farther. Makayla stood in his way. And she was eating toast—*his* toast.

"I caught it when you fell," she said flatly, taking a large bite. "So it's mine now."

Mack clenched his jaw and stomped away. Guilt over messing with the girls' team? So two minutes ago.

"Nice tumble!" Andre said as Mack sat down at the table. The rest of his cabinmates chuckled.

Pat slapped him on the back. "Not your finest moment," he said. "Then again, I don't know if you have one of those."

Mack wanted to scream. He'd already taken a physical beating—he didn't need a verbal assault from a guy who was in on the plan. But a split second before exploding, he realized Pat was just playing his part. In fact, it would've been suspicious if he *hadn't* made a joke about the epic wipeout.

"Good one, man," Mack said, his blood pressure dropping. "Hey, speaking of good ones—want some eggs?"

He pushed his tray toward Pat, who raised his hands in the air. "No, thanks. My doctor said I already have too much sand in my diet."

Mack turned to Andre. "The fall hurt, but it wasn't a total loss," he said, piquing his friend's interest. "I heard the girls talking tactics right before I slipped. We need to figure out how to beat a zone defense."

CHAPTER
11

"WHO NEEDS ALL THAT DRIBBLING AND SCORING?"

A day and a half of practice should have been enough time to prepare for a single basketball game. But learning how to score against a zone defense added a difficult wrinkle, since most of the boys didn't even know what that was.

Mack initially worried he might have to come up with other ways to derail practice, but his fears were quickly relieved. Since he hadn't "overheard" what type of zone the girls were running—there were loads of options, Brian told them—the boys had to learn how to counter all of them.

Five minutes before tip-off in the field house, as Pat, Miles, and other junior campers began filing into the courtside bleachers, the boys were still struggling to learn their roles. They had donned their musty orange pinnies from the storage room and finished warming up, but they had seemingly just begun to argue over who would do what.

"Wait, I thought *I* was running the baseline if they go 2-3," said Elijah.

"No, you're running the baseline if they go 1-3-1," admonished Andre, nervously twisting his A's cap on his head before tossing it behind their bench.

"No! Guys!" Brian said, eyes closed, tugging at his hair. He was crouched in front of them, a play drawn up on his whiteboard in black marker. "None of you runs the baseline, okay? We scrapped that idea."

Brian wiped the board clean with the heel of his hand, clearing away the lesson he actually *wanted* to teach them, and returned to the various setups available to counteract the different types of zone defenses the girls could use.

"Everyone got it?"

Mack watched his teammates nod half-heartedly. They did not get it. And in reality, he thought, they wouldn't need to. But they didn't know that.

The buzzer sounded, signaling the teams to send their starters out to begin the game, just as Winston strode into Mack's view and took a seat in the bleachers behind the boys' bench.

Brian forced a smile. "Okay, good! Then let's get out there. Wi-Fi, Gavin, Andre, Luis, and Mack, you're my first unit. Mack, you take the tip."

"Sure," Mack said. He wanted to seem nervous, so he

made a show of darting his eyes around as he bit a fingernail.

"Take it easy!" Brian laughed. "It's just a game."

Mack let out a breath. "Right. I appreciate—"

But when he looked up, he realized Brian hadn't been talking to him. The coach had a hand on Wi-Fi's shoulder as the point guard shifted nervously on the bench.

"It's just … girls," Wi-Fi stammered.

"You'll be fine, man," said Mack, holding out a hand and pulling his friend up off the bench.

Wi-Fi looked green, but the words seemed to have a calming effect. He took a deep breath. "Thanks, Mack."

"Everybody in!" Brian shouted. "'Avalon' on three! One, two, three …"

"AVERAGE!" the team roared.

In the stands behind them, Winston groaned. No matter how often he heard that pre-game cheer—not to mention the camp's infamous "We're number two!" chant—it seemed unlikely he'd ever get used to it.

The camp's head referee, who doubled as a senior basketball counselor, walked onto the court in his black-and-white shirt, whistle dangling around his neck. He also had a fresh-out-of-the-box game ball under his arm.

"Let's go, teams!" he shouted.

As Nicole, Makayla, and Elena left the girls' bench

along with forwards Mia Lopez and Ana Muller, Mack made a beeline for the center-court circle. He put one foot inside of it and bent low, ready to leap. Makayla, his tip-off counterpart, did the same from the opposite side. Players jockeyed for position around the two centers. Then the ref held the ball out between them and tossed it up.

Mack and Makayla leapt at the same time, stretching their hands into the air, but the ball was thrown too high. They both landed and swung their arms wildly as the ball came down. Mack touched it first but awkwardly swatted it straight back up in the air.

The two centers collected themselves and jumped again. This time, each got a hand on the ball and sent it squirting upward yet again.

"I really like this try-to-get-the-basketball sport they've created!" Pat enthused from the stands. "Who needs all that dribbling and scoring?"

As the ball came down a third time, Mack got his full hand underneath it. He wrenched it backward into the waiting arms of Wi-Fi, the boys' point guard.

"Way to go, Mack!" Brian shouted from the sideline.

Wi-Fi dribbled cautiously up the court, watching for signs of which zone setup the girls had chosen. But as he neared the three-point line, Nicole simply dropped into her stance in front of him. Beyond her, the other defenders zipped around, finding checks and calling out their names.

"I got Mack!" Makayla yelled from under the basket, sneakily grabbing a fistful of his jersey.

Wi-Fi sent Brian a panicked glance that said it all—the girls weren't playing zone defense. And as unprepared as they may have been to play offense against a zone, the boys were doubly unready to play regular offense. They had established no plays, no pecking order, no general system.

After watching a dazed Wi-Fi dribble ten seconds off the thirty-second shot clock, Nicole decided enough was enough. She dove for the ball, but at the last second, Wi-Fi crossed it over from his left hand to his right, and suddenly he had a wide-open lane. He drove down it until Makayla stepped in to block his path.

Wi-Fi looked to pass, but his teammates were standing petrified on the perimeter, so he heaved the ball at the hoop. It rocketed off the top of the backboard as he barreled into Makayla, and both tumbled to the ground.

TWEET!

The ref blew his whistle. "Offensive foul!" he called.

Wi-Fi got up, his cheeks bright red, and ran back on defense.

Makayla took the ball for her team, stood at the baseline, and threw the inbounds pass to Nicole, the team's point guard. She crossed half court, then passed the ball ahead to Mia, who was standing on the wing—being closely guarded by Andre.

Mack watched as the girls realized in unison: *This isn't a zone defense!*

Mia held the ball above her head, looking to get rid of it, while her teammates stood dumbstruck and Andre crowded her. He shot a hand up and knocked the ball loose, then he and three others converged on it at the same time, their arms and legs flailing as they tried to secure possession, until someone's foot struck the ball and sent it flying out of bounds.

Not knowing who had touched it last, the ref simply scratched his head. "Jump ball!" he shouted.

"Because that went so well the first time!" Pat said, laughing.

The teams were two minutes into a thirty-two-minute game, but already it felt like a slog.

After Makayla won the tip, the rest of the half played out as the first two minutes had—with little movement by either team and far more turnovers and miscues than actual shots.

When the first half ended, the score was 15–14 for the boys, and it would have been worse had Andre and Nicole not hit a couple of long-range shots each. Even when substitutions came into the game, nobody was able to find a rhythm.

"What's even going *on* out there?" Andre seethed on their bench at halftime. He took a big swig of water and dumped some over his close-cropped dark hair. "And why aren't they doing a zone?!"

Each member of the team turned to Mack.

He frowned, sweat pouring off his face. "What? Why's everyone looking at me?"

"You said they were running a zone defense." Dillon stepped in to press him, his perpetual frown deeper than ever. "I don't know if you noticed, but they're not."

"What do you want me to say?" Mack asked. "I just told you what I heard when I practically killed myself falling in the cafeteria. I didn't force any of you to learn how to beat a zone. We made that call together."

Andre cast a sideways glance at Mack. Then he shook his head and slammed his water bottle on the ground.

"Blaming Mack isn't helping anything," he said.

Brian nodded. "Andre's right. Let's focus on the game and not on fighting among ourselves. We don't have time to develop a whole new playbook, so let's just try to be smart out there. Move the ball, and move *without* the ball. Make smart cuts. Get open."

But the second half wasn't much better than the

first. The players didn't know each other well enough to improve on the fly, and their offensive rhythm didn't come together. Seeing an opportunity to save face, though, Mack worked hard to secure rebounds off his teammates' misses and scored a handful of short bank shots.

With thirty seconds to play, the score was 31–31. Nicole brought the ball up the court, and Wi-Fi hounded her the length of the floor.

Mack was close to the basket covering Makayla, and Andre was on the wing checking Mia. With twenty seconds left, both Makayla and Ana suddenly leapt into action, running to set screens on Wi-Fi to free Nicole up for her drive. But each girl stopped when she realized the other had the same idea, leaving Nicole stranded at the top of the key.

"Go!" each of them shouted at the other, and so both set screens, one on each side of Wi-Fi, bringing their defenders with them.

With ten seconds left and a sudden scrum of five bodies massing around her, Nicole had nowhere to go. She dribbled backward, then crossed over to her left hand and broke free, dribbling hard for the left wing, with Andre staying between her and the hoop.

Five, four, three, two …

Nicole abruptly came to a two-foot jump stop about fifteen feet from the hoop. Andre flew past as she threw up a desperate high-arcing shot a split second before the buzzer sounded.

Everyone in the room held their collective breath as the ball kissed the backboard on its way down, landed hard on the front of the rim, bounced straight up … and fell through the hoop with a light whoosh.

Game over.

Final score: girls 33, boys 31.

The girls on the bench and in the stands leapt to their feet, shouting and applauding. What the game lacked in … well, *everything*, it made up for with a heart-stopping ending. And besides, now their team was just one win away from representing Camp Average at the Swish City tournament.

Andre hung his head as he walked back to the boys' bench, and Mack ran up to put an arm around his shoulder. The two had finished as the team's leading scorers, but it wasn't enough.

"Good game, man," Andre mumbled. "Sorry about that last play."

Mack had a pang of guilt that landed like a punch. "All good," he said—but it sure didn't feel like it.

CHAPTER
12

"THIS IS WAY TOO COOL"

*W*HAM!

It was 4:00 a.m. when Mack jolted awake. He had spent the evening feeling guilty about the ugly basketball game, fighting the urge to come clean with Andre, and fretting over how their camp director would react. Now this sudden slamming noise confirmed it: they were in for a second year of boot camp. Winston had used that the summer before to knock them all down a peg after a baseball team loss.

Mack clamped his eyes shut and held his breath, waiting for the loud, frenetic ordeal to kick in, but heard … nothing. At least, nothing out of the ordinary. There was no angry shouting or stomping on the floor. No flashlights in his face. No air-raid sirens.

Just a groggy moan from the back of the room.

He opened his eyes and traced the sound to its source: it was Pat, curled up on the floor next to his bed near the large blue ink blot left behind by the obliterated 8 Ball.

"Keep it down," the half-asleep boy murmured indignantly. "Some of us tryin' to sleep."

Pat was still there three hours later when he finally woke up for good. Tightly clutching the blanket Mack had thrown over him, he lay unmoving for ten seconds. Then he reached his hand out, made a fist, and rapped lightly on the floor.

Mack and Andre, already awake, turned to look at him.

"He's up!" Andre shouted.

Pat leapt to his feet, angrily swiping at the layer of dust on his left cheek. "Okay, why was I on the floor?!"

"You mean, you didn't do that on purpose?" Mack asked innocently.

Pat abruptly knelt beside his bed to look underneath. "Aha!" he said. "You put this bed in wrong during the prank! The back legs are sitting on the baseboard. It's on a slant!"

"That's true," confirmed Wi-Fi from the bunk above Pat's. "I can neither confirm nor deny knowledge of any pranks, but the bed's been off-kilter since you made your first accusation."

Pat glared up at his bunkmate. "Why didn't you tell me? And why haven't you fallen off?"

"I sleep flat on my stomach, arms out," Wi-Fi said, "like a skydiver."

"And yet I'm the one who went into free fall!"

Mack and Andre burst out laughing.

"You did this on purpose!" Pat accused.

Hassan rolled over in his bed. "*If* you guys had switched out Pat's bunk, would you have deliberately put the replacement in wrong?"

"Hypothetically speaking?" Mack asked.

"Obviously."

"I don't think so."

"Bonus!" yelled Andre. Then he checked himself. "I mean, hypothetical bonus!"

Pat threw his hands up in the air. Then he spun and walked to the sink at the back of the room. "Such a good prank," he mumbled, splashing water on his face.

After breakfast, Mack and the rest of the boys on the basketball team arrived at the field house to find Brian standing in the doorway.

"Turn around, guys," he said. "We're supposed to assemble by the baseball field."

Okay, Mack thought, *this is* really *it.*

He just didn't know what the particular motivational punishment would be. An epic jog? Push-ups for hours? A monotonous obstacle course?

As the team neared the prearranged meeting spot, he

saw a seventy-two-seat yellow school bus parked in front of the office—and cringed.

Wi-Fi took the words out of Mack's mouth.

"What's Winston going to do?" he asked. "Get us to *push* that bus somewhere?"

If that were the plan, at least they wouldn't be alone. Nicole and her teammates emerged from the direction of the girls' cabins and fell in with the boys.

"Oh, great," Mack grumbled. "This keeps getting better."

Then came the icing on Mack's terror cake. As they walked along the side of the bus, a smiling Winston popped out from behind the far end. He was wearing his usual white knee-high socks and red short shorts, but he also had a black backpack slung over his shoulders and a white streak of sunscreen smeared onto his nose.

The boys' and girls' teams came to an abrupt stop in the dirt road, their feet kicking up a cloud of dust.

"I've got a surprise for you," Winston said, showing his teeth.

He let a few beats pass, then frowned.

"Don't you want to know what it is?"

Mack thought, *No?*

Finally, Nicole took the lead. "Of course! What's the surprise?"

"Thanks, *Nicole*," Winston said. "The surprise is …

a day at the fun park in town. I thought we'd spend the morning playing mini putt, then hit the arcade in the afternoon."

Mack's mouth fell open.

"I figure you guys have been working so hard prepping for the tournament," Winston continued, "that you deserve a bit of a break."

The girls all cheered—they hadn't attended camp the previous summer and therefore couldn't know how unexpected this was—but the boys merely gaped.

A no-strings-attached reward ...

From Winston ...

After the embarrassing way their game had gone?

Not a thing they'd previously thought possible.

Winston pounded on the bus door twice. It opened immediately, and he motioned the two teams and their coaches aboard.

The girls elbowed their way to the front of the crowd and leapt onto the bus, and the boys cautiously followed. Winston seemed to enjoy the skeptical glances he was getting as they climbed up and even returned the favor by casting a cold, appraising eye on Mack.

The camp director didn't—couldn't—know Mack was messing with the basketball teams, but clearly he was on high alert for any sign.

While the girls ripped into a chorus of "The Song That Never Ends," Mack and Andre took a seat together, and Nelson and Wi-Fi grabbed the one behind them.

"You guys believe this?" Mack asked under his breath.

"No." Andre shook his head. "Winston's been on his best behavior this summer, but this is way too cool. I don't get it."

Mack scowled. *Best behavior?* If only Andre knew.

The bus door closed, the engine fired up, and the driver eased onto the gas pedal. Mack gazed out the window as they passed the baseball field and the row of junior-camp cabins, then continued up the winding dirt road through the oak and pine trees.

Then the bus and its twenty-three passengers reached the main road outside of camp. The driver flicked on his left-turn blinker and cranked the wheel, pulling out into the unknown.

CHAPTER
13

"YOU WIN SOME ..."

The yellow bus passed like a spacecraft through the alien landscape of town. Four weeks into his six-week summer vacation, Mack found the sights of car dealerships and chain restaurants as foreign as mysterious rock formations on faraway planets.

"Ooooooh," he heard someone at the back of the bus say, returning him to reality. "There it is!"

The Mega Fun Zone dominated its own parking lot. It was two stories high and a few hundred feet wide—the entire front wall decorated in multicolored neon lights and images of Mega Moose, the fun park's sunglasses-wearing mascot—and that was just the arcade portion. Spilling out behind the main building were separate and beautifully designed areas for go-karts, water slides, and eighteen windmill-laden holes of mini putt.

The bus stopped underneath the giant Mega Fun Zone sign, and the passengers filed off.

"Still worried, Andre?" Wi-Fi asked.

Instead of answering, Andre just stared up at the sign with a look of childlike wonder.

Winston disappeared inside the glass double doors and then popped back out a minute later with a sack of game tokens the size of a beach ball.

"To the mini-putt course!" he shouted, and the girls cheered. What's more, half the boys cheered, too, evidently leaving their misgivings behind in the face of the growing mountain of evidence—Winston really was treating them to a day of fun.

The group grabbed putters and golf balls and waited for counselors to split them into foursomes. Then Mack made the first of several incorrect assumptions about how Winston would turn the trip into a painful character-building experience.

Of course he's going to join my foursome, Mack thought.

But he was wrong. Instead, Winston joined Nicole, Makayla, and Elena.

Of course he's going to spend more time offering tips on everyone else's putting form than actually playing, Mack guessed.

But the camp director smiled and encouraged his way through the front nine, bagging two holes in one along the way. Mack, meanwhile, was too distracted to make even the shortest of putts.

Of course he's going to rub his success in everyone's face, Mack hypothesized.

But Winston didn't even mention his score. Nor did he show a hint of angst when Makayla beat him by a single stroke with a miracle shot on the final hole.

"Good game, Winston!" Makayla said kindly, patting the camp director on the shoulder. "You deserved it as much as I did."

"Ah," he said, waving a hand in the air. Then he added, "You win some ..." before trailing off, the thought unfinished.

Mack got one final surprise in the fun park snack bar—Winston let them eat the greasiest lunch in recorded history—before he decided to stop guessing what the scheme was.

"That ... was ... delicious." Andre patted his full belly. "I didn't even know you could *ask* for triple pepperoni, let alone fit it on a pizza."

The four boys from cabin 13 were slumped back in their chairs, flanking a round white table, and Mack had to reluctantly agree. "The word 'pizza' might not even do it justice," he said. "It was more like a pepperoni steak served on a pastry plate."

"With cheese and sauce in the middle," added Nelson.

Wi-Fi sat up straight, suddenly more than half awake. "There was sauce on there? I didn't even notice."

A large figure rose up and loomed over their table. "Wi-Fi not notice something?" Winston asked incredulously. "A guy with his court vision? I'm not buying it!"

Wi-Fi blushed at the compliment, and everyone within earshot—except Mack, of course—chuckled appreciatively.

Then Winston clapped his hands and rubbed them together. "Video games, anyone?"

The kids cleaned their tables at warp speed and poured into the adjacent arcade. Several hopped onto a row of motorbikes and launched into a mass virtual race, while others fired up pinball machines or jumped onto multicolor platforms for dance battles.

Meanwhile, Mack and Andre gravitated to Pop-a-Shot. The game featured two mini hoops sitting side by side at the end of a pair of long arcade cabinets. There were trays at the bottom ready to spit out mini basketballs. The goal of the game was to make as many baskets as possible—and hopefully more than the player next to you—in sixty seconds.

"Best two out of three?" Mack asked Andre, stepping up to the hoop on the left.

But before Andre could answer, the pair heard another voice.

"I got next."

Mack cringed at the sound of their camp director's voice and looked anxiously at Andre. But his friend was projecting only pleasant surprise.

"Here, Winston," Andre said, jumping back from the game, "take my spot."

Winston slid in front of the right hoop without hesitating. "Thanks, Andre," he said. "I didn't even know they had Pop-a-Shot here. I love this game!"

The statement sounded so false and so prepared that Mack was sure this Pop-a-Shot matchup had been part of Winston's plan all along—an opportunity to put his nemesis in his place.

As Mack stared at the mini hoop in front of him, he felt a brief moment of pride in his ability to see through Winston's good-natured veneer. He knew that when others looked at their camp director, they saw a normal-looking man with an affinity for short shorts. But he saw a robber pirate with chainsaw limbs spitting lava. And he knew his version was more accurate.

"You ready, Mack?" Winston asked, holding up two tokens.

"*Me*?" Mack said, snapping out of it. "No, thanks. I was just looking."

He put his hands underneath the game's wooden frame

and tried to lift it, as if testing how well it was bolted to the floor. "Cool game. Sturdy."

Then a crowd started to form.

"Come on, Mack!" Andre shouted. "Show us what you got!"

"Mack, Mack, Mack, Mack!" the other kids chanted.

His cheeks started to flush as he backed away, but Wi-Fi grabbed him by the shoulders from behind like a boxing trainer.

"You got this, baby!" he shouted.

"I don't know about that," Makayla countered. "Winston looks pretty tough!"

"You're not afraid, are you, Mack?" Nicole teased.

He closed his eyes and rubbed his temples. What was the quickest way to get this over with?

"Okay, fine. One game!" he shouted.

The crowd hooted in praise of the decision. Winston smiled and dropped a token into each machine.

"Countdown from three!" shouted Nicole. "Go on 'Go'!"

"THREE …" the crowd started.

Mack eyed his opponent, who was cracking his neck and knuckles at the same time.

"TWO …"

He felt his stomach gurgle, from either the pizza or the pressure.

"ONE …"

He clenched his jaw and narrowed his eyes.

"GO!"

Mack and Winston mashed their start buttons. The lower tray doors swung open, and a batch of mini basketballs shot out in front of each of them.

Mack grabbed a ball and shot it carefully, holding his follow-through as if on a real basketball court. The ball dropped through the net, and the counter above his hoop jumped to three points.

"Nice one, Mack!" someone shouted.

"Whoa!" yelled someone else, laughing. "Check out Winston!"

As Mack sunk a second ball, he glanced over at Winston's hoop. The camp director looked more like a juggler than a basketball player, taking one-handed shots with both his right and left hands in quick succession.

With balls bouncing off the rim and each other, Winston's method wasn't accurate, but it was fast. Very fast.

Mack saw one ball rattle in to tie the score, and then he turned back to his hoop. Ten seconds had already ticked off his minute, and he'd put up only two shots. He kept to his own style but picked up the pace.

As he settled into a rhythm of one basket for every two shots, his point total climbed steadily.

"Thirty seconds left!" Andre shouted.

By the rising tone in Andre's voice, Mack could tell the score was close, but he dared not look over again and waste even one second. Besides, it was impossible to miss Winston's furious octopus arms in his peripheral vision.

By the time the clock hit the ten-second mark, Mack had amassed forty-five points. But Winston had hit his stride, too.

"It's all tied up!" Wi-Fi yelled.

"I can't watch!" Nelson said.

Mack heaved balls at the hoop now, simply trying to give himself as many opportunities for points as possible. But his accuracy suffered, and ball after ball clanged off the rim or hung around bouncing on it long enough to block another one from going in.

The clock ticked down toward zero. Mack panicked, wound up, and heaved one last ball. It hit the front of the rim hard and ricocheted back at top speed.

Right into his stomach.

"FOOO!" Mack's breath escaped his body in a rush as the buzzer sounded.

The pain caused tears to stream down his cheeks, but thankfully no one seemed to notice either the collision or its effect.

"Good job, you two!" Nicole yelled while the rest of the crowd cheered.

Blinking hard, Mack looked up at his score. Forty-eight points. He'd managed to hit just one shot in the final flurry of action.

Then he looked at Winston's side of the game. His point total was …

Fifty-one.

Winston had won. Mack had lost.

Kind of becoming a theme, Mack thought ruefully, wiping away tears with his sleeve.

Winston, beaming, stuck out a hand, and Mack shook it absently.

"Were you saying something about 'best two out of three'?" Winston asked with a wink.

Mack dropped the camp director's hand and backed away, wanting to immediately blend into the group. He found little resistance. The crowd parted for his exit and then closed ranks again around Winston, who took a bow.

"Okay," he said to his suddenly adoring campers, "who wants to face the champ?"

Not me, Mack thought. *Not now, anyway.*

As he watched Andre and Wi-Fi clamor to take his place, he had to admit that Winston was good at a lot of things. Pop-a-Shot, for one. But also manipulating people ... even Mack's friends.

Winston had used the fun park to try out a new tactic—sweetness—and it had worked perfectly. There was no talking to Andre now, Mack realized. His best friend might as well have been wearing a "Team Winston" T-shirt.

But the camp director's motives hadn't changed. And when sweetness stopped working, he'd just return to his old ways. After all, it was just a few days ago that he was cooking up fake reasons to shut down the pool and the archery range.

So did Mack want to face the champ? No. But *beat* the champ? Absolutely. And to do that, he knew one thing for certain—he had to continue working from the shadows.

CHAPTER 14

"IT WAS ONE DANCE!"

"So what'd we miss?"

Pat looked from Mack to Nelson as they settled around the craft-shop table that afternoon, waiting for a rundown of all that had happened at the fun park. But Mack—none the worse for wear from his self-inflicted gut punch—wasn't interested in rehashing his recent failures.

Seated between her brother and Special K, though, Cassie jumped in to give Pat his answer.

"Winston challenged Mack to a game of Top Shots!" she shouted gleefully. "And then he mopped the floor with him in front of everybody!"

"CASSIE! I told you that in confidence!" Nelson reprimanded. "Also, it's Pop-a-Shot."

Mack's eyes flared at his friend. "So you told her he mopped the floor with me?! Thanks a lot, Nelson!" he said. "Hey, Miles, take a note. Remind me to unsubscribe from this guy's YouTube channels first chance I get."

Nelson slammed both palms on the table and stood up. "You wouldn't *dare!*"

"Guys!" Miles interjected, dutifully taking the note on a random scrap of paper despite himself. "It doesn't matter what happened at the fun park."

"I still want a blow-by-blow," Pat mumbled.

"What *matters*," Miles continued forcefully, "is we don't let Winston get to us. I wasn't there, but I have no doubt he was playing head games with you, Mack. Trying to prove that this is his camp, not yours—or ours."

Mack leaned back in his chair. He didn't really want to fight with his friend, no matter how he'd phrased the recap of Mack's matchup with their camp director. After a few seconds, he turned to Nelson. "Still friends?" he asked.

"Still unsubscribing from my channels?"

Mack pretended to consider it, then smiled. "No," he said finally. "Where else would I get my video game recommendations?"

Nelson and Cassie smiled back, then glanced at each other. "'No one's got game like Nelson's Next-Level Gaming!'" they chanted, quoting the channel's tagline.

"I hate *always* having to be the adult in the room," Pat said, drawing both attention and eye rolls, "but we're burning daylight here, people. Do we even know what the next phase of the plan is?"

"I'm assuming we can't just tell both teams to waste time on some other random basketball strategy," Cassie said.

"No." Mack sat back in his chair. "No one seems to suspect foul play, and as long as we keep Andre and Nicole from comparing notes, I think we're in the clear. But the girls won't even look at me, let alone take my word on anything else."

Special K rubbed his chin thoughtfully. "Kind of limits our options, then—seeing as only you and Miles know any of them."

"Well," Mack said, "that's not exactly true."

He looked at Pat.

"What?" Pat asked.

Miles's face brightened as he picked up Mack's thread. "Remember the camp social at Clearwater last summer?" he asked. "You and Makayla ... ?"

Pat furrowed his brow, searching his memory, then his eyes widened in recognition. "It was one dance!" he shouted. "I doubt she even remembers me!"

"Did you do the silver-dollar trick on her?" Special K asked.

Pat shuffled his feet under the table. "I think so."

"Then she remembers you. Probably as 'that guy with the bad jokes.'"

"Hey!"

"I concur," Cassie said, winking exaggeratedly at Pat. "You'd be a tough guy to forget."

Nelson turned green. "I'm going to be sick."

"Okay, fine!" Pat shouted. "I'm unfunny Prince Charming! How does that help us in this particular situation? And why would she trust anything I said after what happened with the girls and Mack?"

"It's true." Miles grabbed his chin thoughtfully. "You're not very trustworthy."

Pat rested his head on the table. "This is starting to feel more like an intervention than a spy committee. Any other criticisms you guys want to throw out there?"

Cassie put up her hand. "You could change your shirt once in a while."

Pat reared back and screamed.

"Okay," Mack said when Pat finally ran out of breath. "That was helpful. Cath … cathar … DICTIONARY!"

"Cathartic?" Miles asked, searching for Mack's word.

"Yes! Like a big relief. I think we're all better for it. But back to the topic at hand."

Mack fished a folded piece of white paper out of his pocket and flattened it on the table. The other committee members gathered around to find a crude pencil drawing of several squares and rectangles intermingling with a few wavy lines.

"That's … nice, Mack," Miles said.

"Is this part of Pat's therapy?" Cassie asked. "Does he have to tell us what he sees here?"

Now it was Mack's turn to lose it. "Guys! Seriously? This is *obviously* a map of the camp!"

Slowly the group began to make sense of it. The large rectangles at the center of the image were the lodge, camp office, and mess hall. The rows of squares were cabins, and the two wavy lines were the shore and the road through camp.

"Ohhhhh," they said.

Mack snatched the page off the table. "Give me that!" he snapped. "It's clear I did things out of order here."

The others returned to their seats as Mack collected himself.

"I had a thought after Winston singled me out at the fun park," Mack said.

Pat sat upright. "He singled you out? What did he say? Was it mean? Did anyone—"

"*Later*, Pat!"

"This is a great meeting," Cassie said.

"Glad someone's enjoying it," Mack said sarcastically. "Anyway, after Winston singled me out, I thought maybe we could do the same thing to the basketball teams."

"But," Special K chimed in, "how do you single out an entire team?"

Mack finally grinned. "That's where the map comes in."

Early the following morning, in the brief gap between breakfast and the first activity block of the day, the members of Mack's secret committee huddled by the side of the camp office. It was already hot out and only supposed to get hotter, and all six kids were dressed in shorts and T-shirts.

But not everyone in the group was sunny.

"I don't feel so good," Miles protested, clutching his stomach.

"Oh, you're just hungry because Mack barely let us eat before dragging us out here," Pat said.

"Hey," Mack retorted, "no one forced you to wait in the frittata line. You knew we were on the clock. We even synchronized our watches!"

"More like 'watch,'" Nelson said, pointing at Miles's. "Mine is broken. I think the battery died."

"Can you synchronize one watch to itself?" Pat asked.

"No, that's just setting a watch," Miles said, his nervousness at this entire endeavor as plain as the bright daylight.

"Hmm, tell me more about this watch stuff, guys." Cassie mimed a yawn, leaned into her brother, and closed her eyes. "It's *so* interesting."

"Whatever!" Mack said. "It seemed important. They do it in all the movies. But anyway ..."

He brought the map back out and pointed at the square indicating Nicole and Makayla's cabin.

"Let's recap: Makayla is in charge of collecting and distributing the girls' mail, and every day she shows up at the office after breakfast to get it from Cheryl. When she does it today, I want Pat and Miles here," said Mack, pointing at the office. "You go in and ask Cheryl for something—"

"Like what?" Pat asked. "I don't want to go in without a backstory."

"I don't know—like a toothbrush or earplugs. They usually have extras of those things in case kids lose theirs."

"Nelson wears earplugs!" Pat said. "I can work with that."

"Fine, earplugs." Mack checked Miles's watch. "When Makayla's approaching, Special K will give you a signal. You head out the door as she comes in, then turn toward the mess hall. But don't go too far before you deliver your line, Pat."

"Great." Pat smiled. "What's my line?"

"You say, 'Did you hear what Cheryl said? I can't believe there's a college basketball scout coming to the game today!'"

"That's a lot!" Pat whined. "Why doesn't Miles have to say anything?"

Mack looked sideways at Miles, whose eyes were wild and lips were pursed in anxiety.

"Okay," Pat said. "Good point."

Miles's throat gurgled as he made his final plea. "Why are we even doing this? How will thinking there's a scout in the stands affect anything?"

Mack smirked. "Trust me," he said. "There's a big difference between the way people play when they're working as a team and the way they play when they're trying to get noticed. You won't even recognize the players on the court when this news gets out."

"Okay," Miles said, "but what if Makayla thinks it's a prank? Maybe she'll see right through us!"

"That's why we added phase two," Mack continued. "Once you and Pat are clear, Nelson and Cassie come along here."

Mack pointed at the stretch of road between the girls' cabins and the office. "You guys know your lines?" he asked the brother-and-sister duo.

"You're talking to the crown prince and princess of unboxing videos over here," Cassie said. "This is a piece of cake."

"All right, good," Mack said. He checked Miles's watch

one final time, then looked up at its owner. "You okay, man?"

Miles gulped. "Whatever. Let's just get it over with."

"Okay," Mack said, "commence mission."

As Pat and Miles emerged onto the road to head into the office, Mack, Nelson, and Cassie took off in the other direction. Only Special K held his position—ducked down and pressed against the office wall, trying to blend in.

Once Mack's group had reached the back of the office, he split off to the right and his companions split left, ready to circle back along the road to intercept Makayla on her way out of the building.

Mack had had few choices about where to place himself to keep watch over things. He could hang around the other side of the office, but then he'd have to poke his head out and risk being seen if he wanted to get a look at what was going on.

He could stand in the shadow of the mess hall, but that would be so far off he'd barely be able to make out any details—who was talking, how the message was being received, or anything else useful.

So he'd chosen option three: hide in plain sight. He stepped onto the junior-camp baseball field, collected his glove from behind the backstop, and jogged to shallow left field, where he'd have an unobstructed view of the office.

As he came to a stop, Andre emerged from the mess hall with a baseball in one hand and his glove on the other.

"There you are, man," he said, running up. "I thought you got lost or something."

"No," Mack chuckled nervously, "just wanted to get outside."

Andre cocked an eyebrow. "You sure you want to toss the baseball around ... before basketball practice?"

"Definitely," Mack said, putting his glove up.

"Okay, cool. I've been wanting to work my arm out a bit." Andre tossed the ball and Mack barely had to move his glove—which was a good thing. With one eye on the office, he wasn't going to be at his most responsive. But with the sun behind him and Andre looking into the glare, his friend would have a hard time noticing his divided attention.

As Mack flung the ball back, he saw Makayla and her teammate Bea Pires materialize.

"There we go," Mack mumbled.

"That's right!" Andre said, responding to Mack's stray comment. He tossed another ball into his friend's glove.

Mack heard a faint knocking sound as Makayla got ever nearer to the office—Special K signaling Pat and Miles. In another couple of seconds, Makayla would have had her hand on the doorknob ... but suddenly the door swung open and Pat and Miles appeared, turning immediately left as planned. Miles was moving with halting steps, but Pat looked confident as he spoke in a torrent.

"Hey! Ball hog!" Andre shouted at Mack.

Mack flushed and threw the baseball back. "Sorry," he said.

Makayla did a double take as she watched Pat and Miles walk away, but she grabbed the door before it closed and walked inside the office with Bea.

"Almost time to go," Andre said to Mack. "Let me throw a couple of pitches? I'll take it easy on you."

"You got it," Mack said on autopilot, dropping into a crouch and presenting his glove.

Andre threw a slow fastball right into the pocket as the office door opened again and Makayla and Bea started down the road to their cabins, mail in hand. Just then, Nelson and Cassie appeared, moving in the opposite direction.

"Nice," Mack said, throwing the ball.

"How about a curve?" Andre asked.

Mack watched the two pairs of kids with intense focus. Nelson held his stomach, trying to look nervous as he spoke to Cassie, and his sister gently patted him on the back.

Once the kids had passed one another, Makayla grabbed her friend's arm and began talking excitedly. Her body language revealed no hint of skepticism.

The plan—for the first time all summer—was working like a charm.

"Yes!" Mack shouted absently.

"Okay, here it is," Andre said. He adjusted his grip and threw the pitch.

The ball flew toward Mack, but before it reached his glove, it dropped sharply and landed on his right big toe.

Mack's eyes popped open as wide as they could go. He wanted to scream out in pain, but somehow he managed to hold his tongue—he didn't want to draw Makayla's attention. Instead, he clenched his jaw tightly shut, then pulled his right foot behind him and began hopping around on his left.

"Mack!" Andre shouted. "You okay?"

Somehow Mack's eyes opened even wider. He spun toward Andre, dropped his foot, and put one finger to his lips, imploring his friend not to yell. But as his foot hit the grass toes first, it sent a fresh shock wave of pure agony through his body. He flopped flat on his back and began waving at his friend with both hands.

"Mack!" Andre shouted again, much to his friend's chagrin. "What are you trying to say?! Speak to me, man!"

Mack simply closed his eyes and rolled in the grass, realizing he was doing more harm than good.

As Laker approached the ball field for a workout with some mini campers, he saw Andre hovering over a writhing Mack, dropped his equipment bag in the dirt, and sprinted over.

"What happened?" he panted.

"I hit him in the toe with a curveball," Andre said frantically, "and I think it broke his brain!"

Mack's heartbeat slowed and so did his squirming. He looked up and saw that Makayla had long since left the road for the girls' cabins.

"I'm okay," Mack wheezed. He sat up in the grass and grimaced as he delicately unlaced his shoe.

"And the toe?" Laker asked.

Throbbing, Mack thought. But it was worth it. The most important parts of the mission had gone off without any problems.

Which meant that that day's basketball game was going to be full of them.

CHAPTER 15

"QUIT BITING!"

By game time that afternoon, news about the scout had spread like wildfire. And even better for Mack, the rumor had evolved, broken-telephone style, to exclude its actual source.

First Makayla told some kids she heard the news while picking up mail.

Then one of them told others that the camp had received a letter from the college scout.

Before long, kids were talking about how the scout was bringing letters of intent—basically scholarship offers— for the most impressive kids in the game.

Now there were several competing versions of the news, and everyone was suddenly an expert on scout behavior and scholarships.

But one thing wasn't up for debate: there was a far bigger buzz in the gym than there had been for the first game of the series. Most of junior camp had shown up again to fill the bleachers, and kids spoke in hurried, excited bursts.

As the two teams broke into layup lines on opposite ends of the court, each player's attention occasionally drifted to the crowd to see if the mythical talent evaluator had arrived.

But for the moment at least, he was nowhere to be found.

"How's your toe, Mack?" Nelson whispered as they waited for their turns in the boys' layup line.

"It's fine," he said, lying just a little. "Nothing some ice couldn't fix. I told Brian I could play, so we're good."

Then Nelson got to the question he really wanted to ask. "Where's your scout?"

"He'll be here."

Nelson surveyed the stands and saw Pat sitting with Miles, Spike, and Mike. He had his arms crossed and a frown on his face.

"Pat still mad you wouldn't let him pose as the scout? Seemed like he put a lot of effort into his costume."

"I guess so," Mack mused, looking up at his pouting friend. "I just want to know where he got that trench coat so fast."

Then Mack's eyes settled on a different section of the bleachers. In the third row at the far end of the gym, Winston watched with rapt attention as Elena took a three-pointer on the girls' hoop. When the shot hit the back of the rim and bounced away, he smacked his knee like his whole vintage Wheaties box collection had been riding on it.

"Your turn, Mack!" Wi-Fi shouted.

Mack flushed when he realized he was at the front of the layup line with a basketball in his hands. He dribbled down the lane, laid the ball in off the glass, and cycled through to the rebounding line just in time to see the field house door open.

The man who walked in was unfamiliar to everyone in the room. He looked to be about thirty years old and wore a black T-shirt, long black basketball shorts, and new white sneakers. In one hand he carried a water bottle and in the other a spiral-bound notebook with a pen attached.

He quickly found a seat at the back of the bleachers, sat down, and flipped to the middle of his notebook, training his eyes on the court.

Andre grinned at his teammates while he waited for his turn to take a layup. "He's going to write my name in that book," he said, "and underline it like ten times!"

"Fat chance!" Wi-Fi teased. "He's going to run out of ink writing about me."

Mack glanced over at the girls' end of the court, and he could see Nicole and Makayla locked in what seemed to be a very similar conversation.

"You actually got a scout to show up!" Nelson whispered in awe.

"Hardly." Mack grinned. "I asked Laker if he knew anyone, and he said his brother owed him a favor."

Nelson gave a quick bark of laughter. "That's Laker's brother?"

"Shh!" Mack cautioned, checking for eavesdroppers over both shoulders. "If anyone hears us, we're sunk!"

"But what if Winston sees him?"

Mack shrugged. "He can just say he's a scout. Winston would probably love that. It'd mean people were taking us seriously."

Just then, Brian whistled loudly. "Bring it in, guys!"

The coach gathered the team around him and gave a rousing speech, singing his players' praises and imploring them to put the first game out of their minds. But he didn't get the cheers or shouts or backslaps he'd been expecting—Mack could see his teammates were only half-listening, often stealing glances up into the stands.

"So, uh," Brian concluded, perplexed, "get out there and, you know, play hard."

Mack gave a light punch to Andre, who was daydreaming. He made eye contact and did a half nod in Brian's direction, and Andre got the picture.

"Right!" Andre clapped his hands loudly, snapping his teammates out of it. "Let's do this, guys!"

The rest of the players joined in the clapping and then put their hands in for their customary cheer.

"AVERAGE!" they shouted.

The starters took the floor, once again meeting their intra-camp rivals at center court.

The referee tossed the ball up between Mack and Makayla, who timed her jump perfectly and tapped it backward. Nicole caught the ball with a flourish and pointed a single finger at the ceiling. "Number one!" she yelled.

In the stands, Winston beamed as if she were declaring the camp's top-tier status instead of just calling a play.

Nicole dribbled to the top of the three-point line with Wi-Fi backpedaling in front of her. Elena, waiting on the wing, faked hard toward the baseline and then cut back to Nicole, hands up for a pass. But Nicole ignored her.

As Elena dropped her hands in confusion, Nicole looked to Mia on the opposite wing and gave her a quick nod. The small forward beelined to Wi-Fi's side, setting a screen with Andre close on her heels. Nicole dribbled around her and turned her shoulders to drive down the lane.

Andre switched to Nicole even though Wi-Fi fought through the screen and stayed pinned to her side.

Mack, who was in the far corner checking Makayla, saw Mia cut to the hoop, wide open, and put her hand up for the pass. But Nicole didn't even look at her teammate. Instead she pulled up for a jump shot, and Andre jumped with her, easily blocking it.

The ball bounced once before Wi-Fi chased it down.

"Nice one, guys!" Brian shouted from the sidelines as his team streamed up the court. "Just remember to talk out there! Mia was open!"

The boys had blown the defensive coverage, but they still came away with a block because Nicole had refused to pass.

With the girls' team in recovery mode, Wi-Fi dribbled hard toward the hoop, coming level with Mack at the free-throw line. But just when it seemed he might attempt a shot, he brought the ball behind him in his right hand and bounced it hard off the floor toward his teammate.

"Ooooooh!" said the crowd in appreciation of the daring play.

Mack reached for it, but the ball passed high over his head and eventually into the waiting arms of Nicole, who was defending on the wing.

"Awwwww!" came the disappointed call from the crowd.

"A behind-the-back bounce alley-oop pass?" Pat shouted from the stands in disbelief. "This game is crazy."

A minute into the game and both teams were already cracking from the pressure.

"Wi-Fi, man!" Andre shouted. "Make the easy play! I was open for a jumper!"

"You gotta move, Andre! I can't pass it through defenders!"

"Maybe you could just bounce it over them!"

Nicole gave up the ball early, but no one trusted her enough to give it back. She spent the entire possession crowding whoever had the ball, and eventually the shot clock ran down to zero without them even getting a shot off.

"You have to pass!" Nicole snapped at her teammates as they ran back on defense.

Makayla scoffed at her. "You're one to talk!"

"At least you two have *touched* the ball!" Elena shouted.

Andre ran to the baseline and grabbed the ball from the ref. He looked up and saw the girls' team slowly back-pedaling down the court as they sniped back and forth. Then he saw Gavin sprinting past them with his arm in the air.

Andre didn't go into a full-on windup, but he came as close to throwing a fastball as you can get with a large piece of orange leather. He reared back and whipped the ball on a flat arc downcourt … right through Gavin's arms and out of bounds.

"Come on, man!" Andre yelled at the ceiling. "That pass was perfect!"

Gavin threw up his hands. "Perfect for who? You'd have to be an NFL wide receiver to catch a ball coming in that hot."

"Guys!" Mack shouted, both liking and not liking how things were working out. He wanted his friends to play selfishly—he didn't want them to come to blows at center court. "Defense!"

Ana inbounded the ball to Nicole, who charged ahead. Ignoring calls for the ball to her left and right, she blew past Wi-Fi with a hesitation dribble.

"Help!" he called.

Mack stepped up into the painted area, but Nicole spun past him and laid the ball softly into the hoop. As she ran back on defense, she looked up at the stands, where the "scout" was furiously writing in his notebook.

"See?" Nicole shouted. "Just give me the ball and get out of my—"

WHAM!

The point guard slammed into Mia's back, stepping on her shoe and sending them both flying forward in a heap.

"Hey!" shouted Mia. "Watch it!"

Nicole looked desperately at the scout, who was writing something else now. Her cheeks burned with anger.

"You watch it!" she said as Wi-Fi dribbled the ball past her. The boys had a huge advantage with only three defenders back. But instead of looking for an easy layup, Wi-Fi stopped at the three-point line and hurriedly launched a jump shot.

The ball arced high through the air, and all the players on the court watched it fly. It hit the back of the rim before bouncing high up in the air.

Andre and Elena were the first to get underneath it. Their arms and legs tangled as they reached skyward, and the ball glanced off the back of Elena's head and fell to the ground.

Mack did as he'd been schooled and dove for it. He stalled the ball on the ground and tried to wrap his arms around it, but the girls' team wasn't going to give up so easily. Makayla dove down and thrust her own arm between Mack and the ball.

Seeing just a little orange was all Andre needed, and he jumped on top, hitting the floor with one knee and Mack's back with the other.

"OW!" Mack shouted. The ball squirted out and rolled along his arm, where the remaining seven players on the court all took a leap at it. Arms and legs stuck out in all directions, and the ball disappeared at the bottom of it all.

The ref finally blew his whistle. "Jump ball!" he shrieked. "Girls won the tip, so boys get possession."

But no one could hear him over the grunting and shouting of the free-for-all on the hardwood.

"Give me the ball!"

"Quit biting!"

"Whose hair is this?"

But Mack was yelling loudest of all. "My toe! Someone stepped on my toe! I need a medic!"

The ref pulled the players apart and sent both teams to their benches. Andre and Wi-Fi threw Mack's arms around their necks and helped him over.

Brian cleared a spot on the bench, and Mack's teammates lowered him down onto it.

"You okay?" the coach asked.

"Not even close!" Mack shouted.

He yanked his shoe and sock off his foot.

"OOOOOOOOH!" His teammates cringed at the sight of his purple-and-black toe, some hiding their eyes behind their hands.

Brian fished an ice pack out of his bag and passed it to Mack. "Can you move it?"

Mack winced as he waggled the toe. "Yeah."

"Okay, that's good at least—it's not broken. But you're not going back in."

Mack breathed a sigh of relief. He felt bad that his friends would have to return to this horrible game without him—particularly because he'd helped make it that way—but he wasn't eager to put his shoe back on. And the way things had been going, he was already fearing his next injury. What would it be? Sprained wrist? Twisted ankle? Maybe he'd lose an eyebrow?

"Okay," he said meekly, plopping the ice pack down on his foot.

"And the rest of you," Brian continued, turning his focus to the four others who'd been on the court, "this is *not* how we practiced."

The players avoided eye contact. They had no good answer for how bad things had got.

"Sorry, Brian," Andre said finally, looking at his shoes. "Guess we lost our heads for a minute."

"I'll say." Brian looked back at Mack. "Take a page from Mack's playbook and put yourself out there for your team. I mean, try not to lose a toe—"

"Hey!" Mack said.

"But do the stuff it takes to win and make your teammates better—not just what might make you look good. Run the plays, make simple passes, wait for good scoring chances."

"We can do that," said Wi-Fi.

"Okay. Dillon and Nelson, you're in for Mack and Luis. Let's see if getting an extra guard out there changes anything for us."

After a quick cheer, the new five walked out onto the court. Andre and Wi-Fi glanced up at the stands to find the scout still there—and still jotting notes—and it quickly became clear that parts of Brian's speech had been lost on the team.

"Hey, Wi-Fi, let's run the play we learned yesterday," Andre said as the two slow-walked to the far baseline to inbound the ball. "The one with the double high screens."

Wi-Fi shot him a disgusted look. "Oh, you'd like that, wouldn't you? You're the first option!"

Andre huffed. "All I'm saying is we need a bucket, and I can get us one!"

"So can I!" Wi-Fi said.

"Why don't you just get me the ball down low?" asked Dillon, running into the backcourt. "I can take Makayla!"

Gavin was hot on his heels. "Come on, man. She's their best defender!"

"And you could do better?"

The ref blew his whistle. "Let's try to finish this game up before I'm in the old folks' home, huh?" he yelled. "Ball in, or I'll give you a technical foul for delay of game!"

Suddenly Andre and Wi-Fi could see themselves as

everyone else in the field house did—four of them yelling at each other in the backcourt, leaving Nelson alone in the offensive end. He was surrounded by three defenders and looking uncomfortable at the attention.

Mack turned from the court to the crowd. He saw Winston clenching his fists so tightly his fingers seemed entirely drained of blood. Then Mack looked up at Pat, who had stopped sulking and instead was practically bouncing in his seat. He shot Mack an enthusiastic thumbs-up.

"Let's go, Average!" he yelled giddily. "You're doing great!"

On the boys' next possession, they ran Andre's play and he made good on his pledge: he set a screen for Wi-Fi, backpedaled to the three-point line, and caught a pass. In the jumble of bodies and switching defenders, he took two sharp dribbles forward and launched an open jump shot.

It was good, and the boys tied the game at 2–2.

"Yes!" Brian shouted from the sideline. Then Mack heard him mumble, more quietly, "Finally."

As the only two scorers to that point in the game, Nicole and Andre then took it upon themselves to shoot the ball whenever they got the chance.

First Nicole forced her way through double coverage to make a layup.

Then Andre dribbled the entire width of the court

twice before finally backing his defender down and hitting a short hook shot.

Then Nicole missed a three-pointer.

Then Andre made a jumper from the baseline.

By the end of the half, the boys had a four-point lead. The two coaches, voices hoarse from screaming ignored directions, tried talking sense to their angry, unresponsive players. Then they simply left their huddles and chatted with each other at the scorers' table for the rest of halftime.

The room was quiet enough that Mack could hear their every word.

"I've seen better games at the YMCA between total strangers," Brian said.

Tamara shook her head in disbelief. "If I didn't know better, I'd be looking for prank-show cameras. I mean, you haven't seen any, have you?"

The coaches fiddled with lineups in the second half, trying to find combinations that would work together. But that turned out to be impossible.

Without making it official, players on both teams had decided against throwing any passes to their captains. In fact, the only intentional passes thrown were after scoring plays or out-of-bounds turnovers—and the lucky receiver of the ball almost invariably refused to give it up.

The result was an unheard-of amount of dribbling and a ton of steals.

Finally, the scoring opened up as the players' frustration turned to apathy and everyone on defense stopped caring. Why help out someone who wouldn't even pass you the ball?

The mood in the gym lightened a little as the teams traded baskets, but there remained a strange awkwardness that permeated well into the stands. And when the clock ticked down to zero, both teams walked off the court like they'd lost—even though the boys had won by five points.

Mack watched Winston stomp down the bleachers and out of the gym at top speed. As spectators, counselors, coaches, and players followed in his wake, the door swung open several times. Each time it did, Mack caught a flip-book glimpse of his furious camp director.

Winston kicking the base of a large oak tree.

Winston gritting his teeth at the sky.

Winston flushing in embarrassment as he realized exiting kids could see him.

Winston ... gone.

When Mack limped through the door himself, he couldn't spot the camp director anywhere. But he saw Laker and his brother huddled on the near side of the tree Winston had assaulted moments earlier.

"Thanks again, man," Mack heard Laker s
brother.

"No problem! I mean, I even *felt* like a scout i
Think it fooled them?"

"Hey, keep it down!" Laker scolded, quickly looking
around to find only Mack and a few other stragglers.
"Just one question, though. What were you writing that
whole time?"

"Poetry!" Laker's brother said. "I got some great ideas
in there!" Then he paused and said, "Oh, I almost forgot
to ask. How did the game go?"

As Mack hobbled toward the nurse's office for treat-
ment on his throbbing foot, he thought he caught a flash
of red from behind the oak tree. Could it be … the red
cloth of Winston's short shorts? Both he and his heart
stopped. He stared at the tree, but there was nothing there.
He convinced himself that either his mind or the light was
playing tricks and continued falteringly on his way.

The more he thought about it, the more relieved he
was that Winston hadn't heard the two brothers talking.

That, Mack thought, *would have ruined everything.*

CHAPTER
16

"YOU'RE GOING DOWN, MAN!"

Mack iced his toe, then returned to cabin 13 just in time to join Miles at the back of the group heading to the mess hall for dinner. Up ahead of them, Pat and Nelson walked in a small pack with Spike, Mike, and Hassan, but Brian, Andre, and Wi-Fi each walked alone.

Miles started in immediately on Mack. "When your plans don't work, it's bad because they didn't work," he whispered. "But when they do work, it's somehow even worse! How is that possible?"

Mack tried to appear as calm and confident as ever. "I thought it went quite well," he lied.

"You can't be serious!" Miles countered. "The whole point of the plan to stop Winston—the covert committee, everything!—was to be subtle. That was the least subtle thing I've ever seen."

"But Winston can't tie it to us or anyone on either team, so we're in the clear."

"Sure, we've been safe so far, but—"

"And the teams aren't going to get better from here," Mack cut him off. "The players can't even walk to dinner together let alone play together!"

Miles dropped his eyes to the ground. "I just didn't think that's what we were doing. Making our friends hate each other, I mean."

Mack watched Andre and Wi-Fi plodding on in silence. In his mind's eye, he could see them sniping at each other on the court, and the image gave him a dull pain in his stomach to go along with the one in his toe.

"I never intended for the game to get that nasty," he admitted. "But we can fix things. I know we can."

He put his hand on Miles's shoulder. "And here's something that might cheer you up. I think we can disband advanced rocketry."

"Really?" Miles beamed.

Mack nodded solemnly. "I think we've done enough. Last meeting is tomorrow."

"I never thought I'd be happy about a rocketry class getting canceled. But this is the best news I've heard all summer!"

Inside the mess hall, the boys from cabin 13 collected steaming bowls of chili with sides of cornbread and sat down at their table. It was silent apart from slurping and chewing noises, but that wasn't uncommon for chili night.

Then Pat broke the silence.

"Hey, Spike!" he yelled frantically at the twin to his right. "What's that on the ceiling?"

As Spike's eyes shot up, Pat reached stealthily for his cornbread. But Mike caught him by the wrist before he could touch the plate. Then Spike looked down, saw what was going on, and shook his head, smiling.

"Nice ..." he started.

"... try ..." Mike continued.

"... Pat!" Spike finished.

Mack laughed at the normalcy of Pat's lame prank, and he could suddenly see a future where things were back to normal. The third game would come and go in a couple of days, and one frazzled, discombobulated Camp Average team would enter the tournament, only to get ousted right away. Meanwhile, everyone else would return to doing what they wanted. No more scheming, no more secrecy.

And at the end of the summer, no more Winston, Mack thought.

But then the daydream disappeared. Out of the corner of his eye, Mack saw Winston stand up from his table and walk to the front of the room—directly beneath the picture of his championship-winning baseball team.

"Hey, all you junior campers! A big … congratulations," Winston said, almost choking on the word, "to the boys' basketball team for evening up their very tight series with our amazing girls' squad."

He paused for applause and got a small smattering. Everyone there had seen the game, and few thought it worthy of praise.

"As a … reward, I thought maybe we'd have a special evening activity tonight. What do you all say to a camp-wide game"—he paused for effect—"of capture the flag?"

The room exploded in cheers. Capture the flag was a camp favorite, and they played it only once or twice a summer. Pat ran from table to table high-fiving campers. Even Andre and Wi-Fi looked excited.

For once, Mack was grateful to Winston. The distraction of an activity like this could make everyone forget the afternoon's game and move on far more quickly than he had thought possible.

"You might have to stay up a bit later than usual because we need to wait for darkness," Winston continued, "but that just gives us extra time to plot strategies. Speaking of which, I'd like to announce our teams' co-captains."

Mack's alarm bells went off. Co-captains? They'd never had captains for capture the flag before, let alone co-captains.

Winston grabbed a large brown box from his table and pulled out a fistful of blue armbands.

"Leading the blue team will be … Makayla Munroe and our brave warrior from this afternoon, Mack Jones!"

Oh, Mack thought. *Oh no.*

He looked stricken as campers from his table and the ones around him patted him on the back. He craned his neck and saw Makayla taking similar congratulations.

"And leading the red team … Nicole Yen and Andre Jennings."

Andre stood up, arms above his head. Then he pointed at Mack. "You're going down, man!" he shouted jubilantly.

Mack tried to muster a smile, but it wouldn't come. His plan had only intensified Andre and Nicole's mistrust of each other, ensuring they'd keep their distance. But now all that work was going to be undone.

Winston suspected foul play. But how?

Then it dawned on Mack.

The oak tree outside the field house.

The flash of red.

What if Winston had been there after all? He would have heard everything Laker and his brother said, and easily connected it back to Mack. From there he could have checked Mack's schedule, found out about advanced rocketry, and instantly discovered who was in on the plan—and who wasn't.

Which meant more trouble than Mack could possibly fathom.

Now that Andre and Nicole were thrust together, there was a good chance they'd start talking and connect the dots—from Mack joining the boys' team to the zone-defense debacle to the scout showing up just in time to turn them all into selfish gunners.

The one silver lining that Mack could think of? Andre and Nicole weren't friends. In fact, Winston's meddling had made them something closer to enemies. There was a good chance they'd keep their distance from each other, discussing only flag-capturing strategy.

But before Winston walked off, he gave the game one final twist.

"Last thing!" He held up a short length of white rope. "Our co-captains will be connected at the ankle by one of these. It'll be a three-legged race to the flag!"

"Whoooo!" the junior campers teased.

For a split second Mack considered bowing out because of his sore toe, but it wasn't the rope tying him to Makayla that worried him. It was the one connecting Andre to Nicole.

Mack watched Winston leave the mess hall with an

ear-to-ear grin on his face. He knew what that smile meant. Maybe the camp director couldn't cajole a Camp Average basketball team to win a major tournament, but there was another contest: the one against Mack. And Winston would do anything to win that.

Mack had to admit, his plan was brilliant. And Mack's was broken.

CHAPTER
17

"NICE STRATEGY, MACK"

"And ... GO!"

Winston lowered his megaphone as kids in blue and red armbands darted in opposite directions. After making his announcement about the game and the captains, he split every cabin down the middle to create two teams of about sixty members each. From cabin 13, Miles, Spike, and Mike ended up with Mack, while Nelson, Pat, and Wi-Fi were teamed with Andre.

Now it was 8:30, and the day's last light was fading, the overcast sky a darkening gray with just a hint of orange to the west.

As the game began, Winston stood at the base of the hill that led up to the senior-camp baseball field. Everything on the far side of him belonged to Andre, Nicole, and the red team. Everything on the near side, including the junior-camp field and the cabins that bordered it, belonged to Mack, Makayla, and the blue team.

The goal of the game was to grab your opponent's flag and return it to your own zone. If you got tagged in the opposing team's zone, though, you had to stay in a designated jail area there until a teammate came to get you. But then, of course, they'd be setting themselves up to get tagged, too.

Each team had already planted its flags—or more accurately, placed its red or blue bandana on the ground in a visible area within the zone. As team co-captains, Mack and Makayla had placed theirs at home plate of the junior-camp baseball field, which seemed as good a place as any.

But as was often the case for Mack, he wasn't much focused on winning the game. He was focused on winning the war with Winston.

To do that, he needed to end the game quickly by letting their own flag get taken. Or else he needed to stop Andre and Nicole from getting too deep into conversation.

Or both.

Their ankles tied together, Mack (on the left) and Makayla (on the right) staggered back to the safety of their field and got their massive group of teammates to huddle around.

"Okay," Mack said, awkwardly kneeling in the grass, "we've got a half-hour window, and I've seen too many games end without a winner. So let's go on the offensive. When I count to five, everybody charge up the hill all at once."

There was a confused murmur from the team. "Wait, *everybody*?" Makayla asked. "Who's going to guard our flag?"

"Nobody! They'll never expect it," Mack said, trying to seem excited. "They might pick a few of us off, but they won't be able to get everyone. Then we'll get the flag and be back with it before they even realize what's happened."

Makayla snorted. "Or they'll put us all in jail and walk down to grab our undefended flag."

"Okay, fine," Mack sighed. "Maybe we can leave a couple of sentries. Who wants to do it?"

Spike and Mike put up their hands.

"Count ..."

"... on ..."

"... us!"

Makayla smiled. "The job's yours!"

Spike and Mike retreated to the backstop, their heads on swivels looking for sneaky interlopers, while the rest of the group skirted around the row of cabins and plodded up into enemy territory.

"Fall out!" Makayla whisper-shouted. "Quiet as you can!"

Stealthily, the group made its way to the top of the hill, taking cover in a stand of oak trees. Makayla then dropped to her belly, kicking both her and Mack's feet out behind them.

"Hey!" Mack whispered. "Watch the toe!"

Clearly unremorseful, Makayla scanned the area with military precision. She quickly spotted the red flag in a shallow clearing beyond the left field of the senior-camp baseball diamond.

Farther down the left-field line, she saw only Andre and Nicole. They were wrapped in what looked like strategic conversation—and maybe even falling down on the job of guarding the flag.

"They had the same idea we did!" Makayla rasped at her teammates. "We need to get their flag back to our zone before they can get ours back here. Move out! Just try not to draw too much attention in case they left any other guards behind."

The group rose and crouch-walked toward the flag. But when Makayla tried to lift her foot, she found it locked in place.

"We won't be fast enough," Mack said. "Let's provide backup."

While their teammates receded into the distance to the left, Mack and a reluctant Makayla ran to the right.

They ducked behind the field's six-foot-high outfield fence and walked haltingly along its curve.

The fence was the main difference between the senior and junior fields, and Mack had always envied how professional it looked from afar. Up close to it for the first time, he was struck by a desire to reach out and touch it.

"It's cool, isn't it?" Makayla said, reading Mack's thoughts. "My field back home doesn't have one."

"Yeah." He smiled in the darkness, surprised at the sudden kindness in her voice. "Neither does mine."

Mack returned his attention to the ground ahead, which seemed to be coming toward them at lightning speed. Without discussing it, the two had sped up and settled into a three-legged jog, swinging their connected inside legs and their free outside ones in perfect harmony.

The improved technique meant they poked their heads around the left-field edge of the fence before their teammates arrived at the clearing. But Mack wasn't interested in their offensive—instead, he immediately zeroed in on Andre and Nicole, who were still engaged in animated conversation.

"We're supposed to be capturing the flag," Makayla scolded after a few seconds, "not stalking the opposing captains!"

Suddenly, the rest of the blue team burst into view,

sprinting past the backstop and into the clearing before the red team captains could move a muscle.

"They really did it!" Mack gasped, despite his divided attention.

"Yeah, they—oh no," Makayla said.

The blue team—or what remained of it—ran screaming out of the clearing, trailed closely by a few dozen red team members, who had been hiding in the shadows.

It was a trap.

"Save yourselves!" yelled Special K before getting tagged from behind.

"That's for stealing my bunk!" Pat shouted, pumping his fist.

A handful of blue teamers got more than twenty feet from the clearing, but they were quickly gobbled up by reinforcements, who'd been lying in wait under piles of leaves and grass at various points on the baseball field.

"I *thought* it seemed like an odd time of year to be landscaping," Mack mused.

"Whatever," Makayla said. "We gotta get out of here."

The pair turned to walk back the way they'd come, but they immediately ran into Wi-Fi and Nelson. Nelson quickly tagged Mack, leaving Wi-Fi to do the same to Makayla. He reached out his hand, but it stopped in midair as if hitting a force field.

"Go on!" Nelson said.

"*You* go on!" Wi-Fi countered.

Makayla raised an eyebrow. "What, you got a problem with girls?"

Wi-Fi tried to say no, but nothing came out. He closed his eyes and willed his hand forward, but it didn't work. The hand wouldn't move.

Finally, Nelson sighed, reached out, and tapped Makayla on the shoulder. Then he marched the prisoners to the jail in center field, where they joined everybody else on their team aside from Spike, Mike ... and Miles.

"Hey, you guys seen—" Mack said as he and Makayla took a seat in the grass, but he got cut off before he could finish.

"Nice strategy, Mack," one blue teamer said.

"They knew we were coming!" shouted another.

"Nicole and Andre ran circles around you!"

Nicole and Andre, Mack thought, remembering his original mission.

As the vast majority of red teamers ran down the hill toward the junior-camp baseball field, Mack shot a glance over at the opposing co-captains, who were standing shoulder to shoulder at the mouth of the clearing. They were still talking, eyes pointed to the ground.

A minute passed.

Then another minute.

Then *another* minute.

Why won't this game end? Mack thought.

Suddenly, Andre trained a steely glare on the group of jailed blue teamers. He locked eyes with Mack, a hurt look on his face.

The stare-down lasted only a second, though. Nicole tapped Andre on the shoulder and uttered a phrase they could hear all the way in center field.

"Where's the flag?!"

Nicole and Andre frantically hopped around the clearing, trying to spot the red bandana, but it was gone.

Then the loudspeakers stationed around camp crackled to life.

"Attention, junior campers!" Winston's voice boomed. "The game is over, and the blue team … has won."

The jailed blue teamers shrieked in surprise. They high-fived and hugged, danced and dapped, and then took off down the hill. They reached the junior-camp field in a humongous wave to find a small boy holding the red flag.

"Miles!" Mack shouted jubilantly, jogging up to him with Makayla. They were so in shock they hadn't removed their ankle tie. "How did you do it?"

Miles fiddled shyly with his glasses, taking pats on the

back from his teammates. "I was at the top of the hill with the rest of you," he said. "You and Makayla split right and the big group split left, but I stayed right there, hiding in the trees." Miles took a dramatic breath. "When I was sure the coast was clear, I cut straight into the woods and went around the back of the clearing. I saw the red team waiting for us to strike, but it was too late to tell anyone."

Now some counselors, including Brian and Hassan, were crowding in, too.

"After the rest of our team got caught, only Andre and Nicole were left on guard," Miles continued, his face morphing into a grimace. "And … uh, they were a little preoccupied. So I snuck into the clearing, grabbed the flag, and bolted. No one saw me until I got back to our zone."

"That's amazing!" Mack said, full of admiration.

Miles shook his head in disbelief. "It was Makayla's idea. She whispered it to me on the way up the hill."

Mack looked over his right shoulder and nearly bumped heads with a blushing Makayla. Only then did he realize they were still attached.

"Oh! Sorry!" He bent to untie the rope, then noticed the vast majority of red teamers were still hanging around their designated jail area.

"Wait, what happened down here?" Mack said, standing. "Why didn't the red team get our flag?"

Hassan pulled Spike and Mike into the center of the crowd. "I can explain that one."

The cabin 13 counselor said he had been standing by the office as the red teamers came stampeding down the hill to find only Spike and Mike between them and the flag.

"But the twins didn't seem scared," he said, remembering with admiration. "They high-fived, dropped into a bent-knee stance, and moved forward to cover the area a few feet in front of the flag. And you guys had placed it in front of the backstop, so it was blocked from behind."

Mack laughed. "Yeah, that was … unintentional."

Hassan said the red teamers came one by one at first, but Spike and Mike tagged them easily, sending them to jail.

"But then the red team stormed the flag as a group. And the twins just slid back and forth in the dirt, never diving, never leaving their feet, tagging one after another until the jail was full and there was no one left. It was—"

Hassan's recap got interrupted by the squeal of a megaphone.

"Good game, everyone," Winston said with a smirk, "but I think that's about late enough. Back to your cabins now, and lights-out as soon as you get inside."

Mack expected that to be the extent of his announcements, but the director had one more trick up his sleeve.

"Counselors," he boomed, "I want you in the cabins as well to ensure these precious heads hit their appointed pillows. So no going out tonight."

As groans rose up from the counselors, Mack knew that Winston was a step ahead of him yet again. He'd put Andre and Nicole together to share the many ways Mack had been messing with them. On top of that, he'd left zero opportunity for Mack and Andre to talk before lights-out—meaning that Andre would stew on that info all night.

"You coming, Mack?" Miles grabbed him by the arm.

"Sure thing."

The pair trudged across the field to cabin 13, neither uttering another word. For the moment, Mack thought, there was nothing left to say.

CHAPTER
18

"WHAT'S SHAKING?"

Lights-out unfolded just as Winston said it would. The counselors stayed in, and cabin 13 was silent from the moment Brian flicked off the light switch.

Mack slept only in fits and starts, and woke up the next day hoping to accept an earful from his best friend so they could clear the air. But Andre remained quiet—to Mack, that is. He played video games with Wi-Fi and intervened in a heated soccey dispute between Spike and Mike but stayed as far from Mack as possible all morning.

First in the cabin.

Then at breakfast.

Then, during basketball practice, which Mack ran through at half speed. Three-legged jogging the night before hadn't bothered his injured toe, but cutting and jumping on a basketball court proved more of an issue.

Still, he was grateful for a way to pass the time

until the final session of advanced rocketry, so he put his head down and bore the dull pain emanating from his foot.

As soon as lunch was finished, Mack assembled his committee of spies and made for the craft shop.

"Okay, everyone, thanks for coming," he said once everyone was inside.

Crowded around the table, Miles, Nelson, and Pat looked eager for some answers, no doubt having noticed Mack and Andre's cold war. Special K smiled politely, blissfully unaware of what was going on, and Cassie yawned exaggeratedly and dropped her forehead onto the table, already bored.

"This'll be short," Mack began.

But before he could say another word, the door opened.

And in walked Andre.

All eyes turned to him as he found an empty seat between Nelson and Pat, who both looked like they'd forgotten how to breathe.

"Hey, guys," Andre said casually to the group. "What's shaking?"

"Nothing much," Mack croaked. "You?"

"Oh, same. Just thought I'd switch things up a bit." He tilted the yellow bill of his A's cap up and off his face. "So I'm joining advanced rocketry."

Nobody had anything to say to that.

"But," Andre continued, looking around the craft shop at the old, unloved art projects, "where are the rockets? Where's the rocketry teacher?" He made a big show of checking under the table, then quickly reemerged. "You're probably going to need one of those."

Mack stuffed his hands in his pockets, taking his lumps like a kid who'd just been hauled into the principal's office for skipping school.

"See, Nicole and I have a theory. We think advanced rocketry was never a real thing. We got to talking last night, and she said you told her *we* were running a zone defense in the first game. But you told us *they* were the ones running the zone."

Miles summoned the courage to speak.

"Andre, there are things you—"

But Andre cut him off. "That zone stuff ... when you think about it, it seems like a pretty good way to get two teams working on useless things. Seems like something a group *this* creative"—Andre looked around the room again, finally settling on Pat—"could pull off."

The camp's prankster opened his mouth to defend his part in Operation Peel Out, but Mack made eye contact and subtly shook his head.

"Nicole also did some asking around," Andre continued.

"She said Makayla first heard the news about the scout … from Pat and Miles."

He turned his cold eyes on the brother and sister. Nelson looked away while Cassie stared back at him, unflinching as ever. But neither of them spoke.

"He wasn't even a real scout, was he?" Andre said, turning to Mack.

It was clear Andre knew everything. And soon, so would everyone else in camp. The only thing Mack could do was contain the damage.

"No," he said finally. "But I hear his poetry's pretty good."

Andre's nostrils flared. It was one thing to be sure of something and another to have it confirmed.

"I can't believe you!" he shouted. "I can't believe *any* of you!"

Mack leaned forward. "Don't yell at them, man," he said. "It was me. It was *all* me. I talked them into it."

"Nobody had to do it if they didn't want to," Andre muttered.

Mack gulped, knowing what he had to say to save the others. "I badgered them. I guilted them. I made them see it my way—just like I did with you last summer. Think about it. Did you really *want* to lose all those baseball games on purpose?"

The entire room seemed to tense up all at once. Andre

glowered at Mack, his anger coming off him in waves. Just when it seemed he might explode, he dropped his eyes to the table. "But why?" he asked. "Why'd you have to mess with the basketball teams?"

Mack shrugged. "To stop Winston. I know you don't believe me, but he really was shutting down parts of the camp in order to—"

"Save it!" Andre shouted. "This one's older than Pat's silver-dollar joke."

"Hey," Pat protested, weakly.

Andre sat quietly for a minute.

"Just one more thing I gotta know," he said, tapping his fingers on the table. "Why didn't you include me?"

Mack's heart sank through the craft-shop floor. The truth was he hadn't wanted to hurt Andre by asking him to sabotage his own team again. But he knew that now wasn't the time to tell that side. Andre wouldn't buy it.

"I guess I just didn't think you'd help."

"Well, you were right about that at least!" Andre shouted. "I wouldn't have!"

He abruptly pushed his chair from the table and got up. Then he scanned the faces in the room, wrestling with a decision. Finally, he waved his arm and made for the door.

"Come on, guys," he said to everyone but Mack. "Let's get out of here."

Nelson, Miles, and Pat stole quick looks at Mack, who just nodded solemnly, urging them to go on. Even if they still believed in their fight against Winston, none of them could prove the camp director had done anything. They'd also gain nothing from giving the cold shoulder to Andre.

Slowly they all stood and walked past Andre out the door as Mack remained seated, slumped way down in his chair.

Then Andre shot a single withering glare at Mack.

"Probably goes without saying, but you can forget showing up for basketball practice," he said. "Not that you ever wanted to be there anyway."

Andre stepped outside with the others and let the door slam behind him.

Suddenly alone in the empty room, Mack worried less for himself than for his friends. Would they be able to get past this?

As it turned out, he didn't have to wait long for an answer.

"Hi, Andre," he heard Cassie say. "I don't think we've properly met. I've heard *so much* about you."

A palm smacked against a forehead. "Not *now*, Cassie!" Nelson shouted.

Mack listened as his friends' laughter receded down the hill. At least his plan hadn't ruined *everything*.

CHAPTER 19

"HE DID *WHAT?*"

Mack was able to stare at creatively painted horse-head bookends for only so long before he got bored and left the craft shop with a sigh. He had developed serious doubts about both his scheming abilities and his understanding of potential side effects, but he still knew Camp Average. He was sure news of his treachery would already be spreading like an airborne virus. A whisper here, a nudge there, and pretty soon everyone—from mini campers to counselors—would know him as the guy who'd tried to submarine his own basketball team.

While Mack mainly wanted to curl up into a ball and lick his various wounds—both physical and emotional— there were still several hours before dinner, and he had to go somewhere. And because of camp regulations, he needed to let someone official know where that would be.

He picked the shortest possible path down the hill toward the office and made for it at top walking speed.

On the way, he encountered just one group: a counselor and four mini campers holding comically oversized tennis racquets on their way to the courts.

They didn't seem to notice Mack as he walked by them, but before he was out of earshot, he heard a whispered question.

"He did *what*?"

Mack smiled weakly as he realized how absurdly that conversation would play out. From the outside looking in, his plan would seem strangely cruel, but it would also be confusing. If there was an upside to all this—and it was a tiny, obscure one—Mack suspected his camp as a whole was about to become more knowledgeable about the finer points of zone defense than some professional basketball teams.

A minute later, Mack pushed open the office door and stepped inside. Catching the door before it could slam behind him, he surveyed the room. Cheryl sat typing an email on her laptop, her hands flying across the keyboard.

"Uh, hi," Mack whispered as he approached. He felt drained, as much from lack of spirit as lack of energy. "I need to update my schedule."

Cheryl tapped the trackpad hard, sending her email with a flourish, then swiveled her chair toward Mack.

"No loud declaration this time?" she asked, teasing. "That's not like you."

Mack forced a smile. "Guess that was a one-time thing," he said.

"What can I do for you? You adding something else?"

Mack's mouth felt suddenly dry, as if all the water in his body was preparing to escape out his tear ducts. "I need to drop advanced rocketry ... and basketball."

Cheryl looked Mack in his misty eyes.

"Are you sure?" she asked. "Is anything wrong?"

"Yes," he answered, drawing an inquisitive look from the administrator. Then he realized his error. "No! Sorry. I meant yes to the first question, no to the second. I'm fine. Just looking for a change."

Mack heard the words coming out of his mouth as if he were standing in some other part of the room. Who was this odd person who wanted a change? No one at Camp Average wanted change. No one except Winston.

"Okay, well, we can take care of that."

Cheryl swiveled back to her computer, clicked through some folders, and opened a spreadsheet containing Mack's schedule. She deleted the basketball and advanced rocketry blocks, leaving the page bare.

"So what do you want to do?"

Mack reddened.

"What, like ... now?"

"Well, yeah." The corners of Cheryl's mouth turned

up. "Now and the rest of camp. We've got a week and a half left. Your days are empty. What do you want to transfer into?"

"I don't know." Mack scratched his head. "Guess I hadn't got that far."

He turned away from Cheryl while he thought over his options. He didn't need a brochure to inform himself of the possibilities—he knew the brochure by heart—but he had trouble deciding which to choose.

Basketball was obviously off limits. Baseball was finished for the season, and advanced rocketry was canceled. Mack suddenly, desperately wanted to sign up for the real version of rocketry, but he didn't want to incriminate Miles any more than he already had. His friend had tried to talk him down to smaller plans, but he'd pushed ahead anyway and managed to ruin everything. He had lost at least one friend, made it so he couldn't see several others without getting them in trouble, and turned Winston into the good guy—the kind you compete hard for, not try to take down.

And no matter how much he wanted to strap on a life-jacket and hop in that speedboat he kept missing, he just couldn't see himself sitting tightly packed with a group of kids who'd heard he was a monster. He also imagined they'd throw his towline overboard the second he got up on skis.

Every activity seemed to involve a group of some sort. So where could he be with others but alone?

Where could he salvage what was left of his time at Camp Average, his favorite place on Earth?

The answer washed over him all at once. He turned back to Cheryl and tried an altered version of a question he'd shouted at the sky at the start of all this.

"Could I just go swimming?"

Mack pulled his goggles over his eyes and toed the edge of the pool deck. Then he dove off of it—leading with his hands, tucking his head to his chest, and plunging beneath the surface. He kicked his feet behind him and pulled his hands back and to his sides, trying to maximize his underwater distance—not to mention his time in the absolute quiet and anonymity of the bottom of the pool.

Mack had signed up for intermediate swimming techniques in the mornings and advanced ones in the afternoons, both of which essentially amounted to doing as many laps as you wanted under the watchful eye of lifeguards who would help only if asked. Despite Winston's efforts to make swimming a more competitive activity, he hadn't found any camps to challenge and so pretty much left it alone.

Breaking the surface of the water, Mack turned his head to the right, took a deep, loud breath, and began his freestyle stroke. He furiously pulled at the water ahead of him, one arm after the other, until he reached the pool's opposite side.

After four lengths, he took his first break. He rested one arm on the wall, ripped off his goggles, and gulped for air.

He refused to scan the pool for signs of how he was being received by his peers, but as his breathing died down, he couldn't help but hear a few barely whispered words.

"I can't believe he would ..."

"Heard he hired an actor to play the scout ..."

"Who slips on a banana peel?"

Mack yanked his goggles back on and kicked off the wall. He swam until his arms and legs ached, and his lungs felt deflated. And by the end of the day, he didn't need to fake sleep to sidestep hard questions. He was legitimately exhausted, falling asleep as soon as his head hit the pillow and staying asleep until it was time to leave the cabin for breakfast.

Avoiding eye contact with everybody but the servers at the steam table, he ate quickly and disappeared at the earliest opportunity. Then he made his way across the field without once looking up from the ground.

Just need to get to the pool, Mack thought. *So long as it's still there.*

He had a nagging worry that Winston had closed his swimming refuge overnight, but the pool was staffed and full of water upon his arrival.

And that's when he realized that Winston was done with him.

The camp director had planned and plotted, prodding him into a rematch battle of wits. Now it was over—Winston had won, hands down—and Mack was free to finish his summer at the pool.

There are worse fates, he thought.

There was only one remaining hurdle: the final basketball game that afternoon. To Mack's utter horror, everyone in junior camp had to attend. Including him.

CHAPTER
20

"YOU BRING MY BED?"

The layup lines were at full speed and the stands nearly at capacity by the time Mack walked into the field house with a group of afternoon swimming kids. His hair was wet and falling over his forehead in tangles, and his eyes were hidden behind a pair of black plastic sunglasses with fluorescent yellow arms. He wore a green T-shirt and damp swim trunks, and had a towel slung around his neck. To anyone observing, his appearance sent a very clear message: *Don't worry, I'm just passing through.*

Out of the corner of his eye, he saw Miles on the boys' bench, a raft of papers in his lap. He had kept stats for the baseball team the summer before and had evidently got the call for the basketball team as well.

Mack ambled up the bleachers, an impassive, uninterested look on his face, and took the same seat Laker's brother had—the last possible one in the last possible row. There were a few spaces between him and the next kid, and he was sure they'd stay empty.

But they didn't. Not for long.

Two minutes before game time, Pat came down the row, stepped awkwardly over a bunch of junior campers, saying, "Not sorry, not sorry, *definitely* not sorry, don't excuse me," and sat next to Mack without looking at him.

"What are you doing here?" Mack said.

Pat feigned surprise. "Oh, hey, didn't see you there!" he said. "How's your new job going?"

"What job?"

"The acting gig where you play someone trying to blend in at the beach. Your costume is great." Pat looked him up and down approvingly. "But you forgot the strip of sunscreen. Let me help you."

Pat exaggeratedly licked his thumb and prepared to rub it down Mack's nose, but Mack pushed him off.

"Get *off*, Pat!" Mack laughed despite himself.

All around them, their fellow campers turned to look.

Mack forced a cold expression. "I mean it, man," he whispered. "You don't want to be seen with me. You gotta go. Like now."

"No problem," Pat said, but instead of moving, he turned his gaze up the row, where Special K was climbing over kids to get to them.

"Hey," Pat said when his friend sat down. "You bring my bed?"

Special K ignored him and leaned toward Mack. "What's up?"

Mack dropped his head into his hands. "Same old, same old," he said. "You guys are just killing me."

But the floodgates had opened. Still basking in their newfound capture-the-flag fame, Spike and Mike high-fived everyone in the row on their way to joining the group.

Finally, Cassie walked along the sideline of the court until she was directly below them. She then climbed straight up the stands, parting the seated kids on her way, and squeezed directly between Pat and Special K.

Now the row was so full it could barely contain them all, and Pat was pressed up to Mack so tightly he nearly pushed him off the bleachers altogether. Despite that, Mack had a sudden feeling of invincibility. With friends like these, who feared anything?

Cassie gave Mack a once-over. "Is this a stakeout?" she asked. "You look like an undercover cop."

"That's what I told him!" Pat shouted.

Mack rolled his eyes beneath the sunglasses, which he now planned to wear to bed just to spite them. "Thanks for coming, guys," he said, trying but failing to sound sarcastic. "No—really."

Down on the court, the ref blew his whistle and the starters left their benches.

Dillon beelined it to the center circle to take the tip for the boys' team, while Makayla took her time in getting there. The two dapped fists and bent low, their hands raised and ready as their teammates set up around them.

The zebra-striped official briefly held the ball between the two centers. But from where Mack sat, neither seemed to be looking at it—instead, each player was focused on the other.

This is going to be brutal, he thought.

A hush fell over the field house. The ref threw the ball in the air and ...

Nothing.

The ball reached its peak high over the hard court and dropped down to Earth without anyone on either team moving a muscle. It bounced once, twice ... twenty times before finally rolling along the center-court line toward the players' benches.

Winston stood from his spot in the bleachers. "Very funny, guys. Let's play some basketball."

He climbed down, picked up the ball, and looked for someone to throw it to, but only the ref raised his hands.

"Are you forgetting something?" Winston asked the

players irritably. "You need to play to see which team gets to go to the Swish City tournament."

Andre stepped forward. "No, we don't."

"What are you talking about?" Winston snapped.

"If we're going to the tournament at all, we're going as one team," Nicole chimed in. "Girls *and* boys."

Mack's jaw dropped. The kids in the stands cheered enthusiastically.

"That's not possible!" Winston silenced the crowd. "It's too big a team! The tournament rules would never allow it!"

Miles stood and held up the pages in his hand.

"Actually," he said, his voice confident, "that's not true. The tournament rules say nothing about roster size, so there's nothing stopping us from taking twenty or thirty or even fifty players."

Winston was shaking with anger. "Fifty players?!" he blurted, pulling his hands through his hair. He opened his mouth to continue speaking, but another voice stopped him.

"I think it's a great idea!"

It was Laker, standing tall in the bleachers.

"But—" Winston stammered before again getting cut off.

"Me, too!" shouted Tamara.

"BUT!"

Brian started clapping. "Best idea ever!"

Pretty soon the entire crowd chimed in—shouting or clapping or stomping, or all three. And the volume only increased as Winston stormed past Laker and out of the field house.

When the cheering finally died down, Brian cupped his hands around his mouth to address the crowd. "Time to go, everybody. The basketball teams—"

"Team," Nicole corrected him.

"The basketball *team* has *a lot* of work to do."

Mack filed down from the stands with his campmates. He had just reached the door when he heard someone call his name.

"Hey, Mack!"

He turned and looked back, his hand on the door-frame. Andre was standing in the middle of the court, a ball trapped between his hip and forearm.

"Where d'you think you're going?"

CHAPTER
21

"WHAT CHANGED?"

Two minutes later, the only people left in the gym were Brian and Tamara, who stood outside the equipment room, where their collective twenty players plus one—Miles—had gathered. There was barely room to breathe inside the small, musty space, and yet Mack stood alone, a full couple of feet from the nearest person. He blushed, still refusing to take his sunglasses off, wondering what he was doing there.

"I'm assuming there's a reason you brought us in here, Andre?" Nicole asked.

"Tradition," Andre answered cryptically, though the members of cabin 13 knew what he meant—this was the site of all their plotting against Winston the previous summer. What it lacked in comfort, it made up for in seclusion.

"But also," Andre continued, turning to Mack, "there are some things we need to discuss."

Here it comes, Mack thought. *The final confrontation.*

"I'm still mad at you for the way you handled ... well, everything."

"You tricked us into doing stupid stuff that made us fight among ourselves and look bad on the court," Nicole chimed in.

"And now that scout will never say nice things about us!" moaned Dillon.

"That scout wasn't real!" yelled Luis. "How many times do we have to tell you that?"

Mack stared at the floor as all this was going on, but he could feel others inching even farther away from him.

"But," Andre continued, his voice softening, "I know why you did it. And I get it. And I'm sorry for not hearing you out when you tried to talk to me earlier."

Mack raised his head abruptly. "Huh?" he grunted.

"Winston," Andre said. "You were right about Winston."

"I'd heard that guy was a piece of work," Nicole said, "but I didn't know the half of it. *Somebody* had to try to take him down."

Mack looked at their faces as if trying to solve a math problem from two chapters ahead in his textbook.

"But ... what? Why? How?" he stammered. Then he took a deep breath. "What changed? Why do you believe me now?"

Andre looked around until he saw the sleeve of Miles's

T-shirt poking out from behind a pack of players. He grabbed it and pulled the blushing boy into the center of the room.

"Turns out the rocket scientist makes a good defense attorney."

Mack choked up. "Miles?" he asked. "You stuck up for me?"

"Oh, he didn't *stop* sticking up for you." Andre smiled. "Not once over the past two days has he talked about anything else. He said that you were right about Winston, and you were only trying to help."

Makayla spoke up. "Nelson and Cassie came to speak to me, too."

Mack spotted Nelson sitting on a ball-hockey net. "Thanks, New Money."

"It was nothing," he replied quietly.

"Hardly!" Makayla scolded before returning her attention to Mack. "They apologized for tricking me with the scout talk and insisted that we not blame you for all of it. Cassie called Winston an evil mastermind—and a bunch of names I can't really repeat."

"Sounds like Cassie," Mack said, grinning.

"And Pat cornered me in the mess hall this morning," Nicole said. "At first, he mainly wanted to talk about silver dollars ..."

"Figures," Mack said, shaking his head.

"But when I asked about you, he got all quiet. He just said, 'Mack's a good guy. He doesn't deserve the crap he's getting.' And that's when I realized—I already *knew* that. If you were willing to stick your neck out for something, you had to have your reasons."

"We still needed evidence to back you up, though," Andre chimed in. "And that's where Wi-Fi came in."

"Wi-Fi!" Mack said, instantly conjuring the full story in his head. "You hacked Winston's computer!"

"No," said Wi-Fi, stepping into the patch of floor that Miles had vacated. Then he tapped his lips, suddenly lost in thought. "I mean, I guess I *could have* …"

"Ten bucks says his email password is 'Winning,'" Andre mused.

"But it was way easier than that," Wi-Fi finished his thought. "I just asked Cheryl."

Mack furrowed his brow. "Cheryl? Really?"

"Think about it. Winston closed the waterfront because there was the itch. He closed the pool because it had a leak. He closed the archery range because it had an ant infestation. To fix all that stuff, he'd need to book a water-cleaning company, pool-maintenance people, and exterminators—and all those things go through Cheryl. But when I asked her about it, she kind of said, 'Huh,' realizing how weird it was. Not only did she not have to call anybody, but not a single person showed up to fix anything."

"Winston didn't call anyone because he made up all those problems," Andre said. "He was messing with us—with *all of us*—again. And you were trying to stop him."

Mack noticed the gap had closed between him and the rest of the room.

"And to think I played Pop-a-Shot with that guy!" Andre continued. "And I was cheering for him when he played you!"

"WHAT?!" Mack shouted.

"Guys!" Nicole interrupted. "Focus!"

The room came to an immediate quiet, making it clear once again why she was a natural captain.

"I love the idea of one team," she said, "but does it even work? Also, should we even be entering the tournament?"

"What do you mean?" Mack asked.

"If we enter," Nicole replied, "we'll do our best, right?"

"Right," Mack said, looking at Andre.

"And if we do our best, there's a chance we'll win, right?"

"Right!" chanted the rest of the kids in the room.

"Well, if we play for Camp Avalon and win, then so does Winston. And everything you guys did and we just went through would be for nothing."

The room again fell silent.

Then Nelson hopped off his hockey net.

"I just had an idea about that," he said, seeming far more like his YouTube self than he ever had in their presence. "What if we're not playing for Camp Avalon?"

CHAPTER
22

"BIT OF A SHAKY START THERE"

"For those keeping score, this team now has two head coaches, twenty players, and two captains," Brian said. He and Tamara stood on the court as they addressed the team, which took up the full first row of the middle section of the field house stands.

"There's only one way a team this big is going to work," said Tamara, "and it won't be everyone's idea of fun."

This was an out, and the players all knew it. But not a single one blinked.

"What's your idea?" Nicole asked matter-of-factly.

"Essentially? The exact opposite of what we've seen from you so far," said Brian.

Tamara nodded. "If you want everyone to play and the team still to be in any way competitive, we have to treat this more like hockey than basketball."

Miles raised his hand.

"Yes, Miles?"

"Uh, I didn't see anything about roster size in the tournament rules," he said warily, "but I think they'd frown on body checks and wooden sticks."

Tamara snorted. "What I mean is, we'll have players expending maximum effort at all times on both ends, like in hockey. And we'll sub players on and off five at a time, like in hockey."

Mack thought for a second. With games that consisted of four eight-minute quarters, this plan meant that each player would get one four-minute shift in the first half and one in the second.

He couldn't help but wonder: How would a team that had lost its collective head over the idea of a scout in the stands handle a strategy like this? There might actually *be* scouts at Swish City—for elite prep teams instead of colleges—but no one would be on the court long enough to get noticed.

"There'll be no over-dribbling, no ball watching, no taking possessions off," Tamara continued. "No one plays big minutes. No one gets all the glory."

"And the kicker—" Brian started.

"So we're playing football now, too?!" yelled Nelson.

The other members of the team laughed. Nelson hadn't intended it as a joke, but it was one Pat would've appreciated.

"No," Brian said, "still talking basketball. The *final item on our list* is we're going to run a full-court press."

Mack knew what this meant—when most teams play defense, they guard opposing players only near their own basket. But running a full-court press means defending the entire court at all times. In other words, it's exhausting.

Elena raised her hand. "Like, we're going to press sometimes?" she asked.

"We're going to press *all the time*. Every time the other team inbounds the ball in their own end."

Brian and Tamara crossed their arms in unison, as if resting their case.

"How's that sound?" Tamara asked, raising an eyebrow.

Andre locked eyes with Nicole, then he craned his neck to look at every member of the new team. Mack followed his gaze. He didn't see reticence on the faces of his teammates—not to the strategy or to the sound of hard work. He saw determination.

Andre turned back to face his coaches. "Sounds perfect," he said.

"Okay, good." Brian smiled. "Let's get started."

The tournament was four days away. With an hour to go before dinner, the team's two coaches decided to start their seemingly impossible task with something simple: defensive stance.

"If we're going to stay in front of ball handlers over the length of the entire court," Tamara said, "we'll need a refresher on defensive slides."

Nelson put up his hand. "Refresher? I don't even know what they are."

"I'm sure you do," Brian said. "Have you watched any professional basketball?"

Nelson shook his head.

"College basketball?"

"No."

Brian racked his brain and found the closest example he could think of. "Were you on the blue team or the red team during capture the flag?"

The coach got multiple confused looks, but Nelson answered, "Red team."

"Then you were there for Spike and Mike's epic tagging session. Minus the actual tagging, *that's* what you need to do to keep a player from getting to the hoop."

Nelson made a face like he'd just walked into a stinky-cheese shop.

"I know—it's weird, and I have no idea if they were doing it on purpose, but they were executing textbook defensive slides the entire time. They stayed low, they pointed their toes, and they never crossed their feet. They didn't dive, they didn't overcommit, and they stayed balanced. And nobody got past them."

Brian demonstrated by dropping into a crouch and dancing side to side, taking a lunging step with his lead leg and dragging the other one behind him.

The red teamers who'd rushed the blue flag during the game—Nelson included—had a moment of recognition.

"No wonder we couldn't get by them!" Elijah yelled. "They're defensive geniuses!"

While Miles tucked into a book called *Optimal Basketball Record Keeping* on the sidelines, Tamara arranged the players in loose lines and had them slide as one around the court. Though the constant crouching made their legs ache, the players all picked up speed and shortened their reaction time, getting used to changing directions quickly.

After twenty minutes of this, the coaches called for a water break and grinned at each other. Maybe this wouldn't be as hard as they thought.

"Let's put that into practice!" Brian yelled.

The two coaches split the group into four random five-player teams and directed two to each basket. The teams given orange pinnies were asked to play defense, and the teams in yellow got the ball.

The coaches positioned the offensive players in a standard setup—three players around the three-point line and two players on the low blocks. Their defenders each stood between them and the basket.

"Okay, looking good," yelled Tamara so she could be heard on both ends of the court. "Yellow teams, we're just running a simple motion offense. Pass and move."

"And remember: We don't want *good* shots. We want *great* ones," Brian added. "We want shots near the hoop and wide-open three-pointers, if you're comfortable with them."

"Wait," Nelson said. "Three-pointers? Aren't those, you know, harder than other jump shots?"

"Yeah," Brian said, "but not by much, and the potential reward of the extra point makes it worth it. Plus, it'll space defenders out and give us room to move inside."

Nelson seemed satisfied with the answer, and Tamara picked up the thread.

"If you don't have a great shot, don't worry," she said. "Just pass the ball to an open player and get open again or set a screen to get someone else open. Make the right play. No standing around."

Mack's teams back home had always relied more on set plays, but this strategy made sense given the lack of practice time. It also ensured they'd pass the ball.

"Orange teams," Brian added, "move your feet on defense. Stay in front of your checks. Switch screens and talk."

At his end of the court, Mack was on offense with Nicole and Omar, as well as two other players from the girls' team, Kristi Lloyd and Jewell Toliver. Nicole slapped the ball to start the play, and Mack crossed the key to set a screen—only to immediately bump into both Jewell and Omar, who had the same idea.

"Oof!" Mack grunted.

As Kristi caught a pass from Nicole on the right wing, Mack's defender, a forward named Diana Moore, got hung up in the jumble of bodies under the hoop. He made a sharp cut to an empty swath of court at the top of the arc and presented himself for a pass.

Kristi looked at him but froze.

"Who's got Mack?" Brian yelled. "Talk on defense!"

Diana threw her hands up. "I thought we were switching screens!" she yelled at Dillon, the other post defender.

Dillon started running to close out on Mack, who clapped his hands. "Kristi!" he yelled.

But instead, Kristi threw the ball across court to Nicole, and Dillon, suddenly in the middle of the action, knocked it away and out of bounds.

Mack looked at Kristi, who immediately went on the offensive.

"Coach told us to make the *right* play," she seethed. "How am I supposed to know if you can take threes? Aren't you a center?"

"Okay, cool it, yellow team!" Brian said. "Bit of a shaky start there. But it's all good. Let's run it again."

But running it again didn't help things on either end of the court, no matter which team had the ball. Nobody was tricking the players into playing badly anymore. Nobody was messing with their heads. They just hadn't played together—and it showed.

Soon the players heard the dinner bell ring out across camp, and they slumped to the sidelines for a final drink of water.

"We don't know each other," Andre said.

Nicole agreed. "Even worse, we don't *trust* each other!"

"If only Spike and Mike had put on an accidental motion-offense clinic, too," Makayla joked, trying to lighten the mood.

But Andre was somber as he chugged back his water. "The way everyone's talking about it, I'm kind of bummed I didn't get tagged by those guys. I didn't even see it. I was up on the top field, tied to Nicole."

Mack felt embarrassed—they'd somehow stumbled

into a conversation about the moment Andre and Nicole had discovered his treachery against them.

But then something else in the memory took center stage. And it gave him an idea.

At that exact moment, Brian let his frustrations boil over. "We don't have time for this," he whispered to Tamara.

Before Mack could stop himself, he blurted, "Maybe we don't need it!"

The gym went dead silent. Mack hadn't intended to draw so much attention, and suddenly he wished he hadn't said anything at all.

"What was that?" Brian asked.

"Nothing," Mack said, trying to wave it off. "Sorry. I'm not a coach or a captain. And I know you've all had more than enough of my ideas for one summer."

Nicole wiped sweat from her brow with her forearm. "I don't know about that," she said.

"Your ideas are crazy," Makayla added, "but they can be ... oddly effective."

"Yeah, Mack," Andre said. "Let's hear it."

Fifteen minutes later, the twenty members of the newly unified basketball team walked into the mess hall in blushing, lurching pairs. They were late for dinner, which meant the rest of the campers were already seated—and in prime gawking position.

Walking shoulder to shoulder with Shona Gaucher, a curly-haired center, Mack watched as whole tables of kids dropped their gazes to the basketball players' feet.

And what they found there was a wholly unexpected sight.

"They're tied together!" someone shouted.

It was true. Each boy–girl pair was connected at the ankle by a short length of rope, just as the capture-the-flag co-captains had been.

"The team's so big they're trying to sneak ten players onto the court at the same time!" said one camper.

But the players were evidently in no mood for joking and stared straight ahead—except for Wi-Fi, who looked at the ceiling in an effort to ignore the constant physical contact with the girl at his side.

The players had accepted Mack's idea, but only grudgingly. Few were chomping at the bit to be tied to someone they didn't know, but no one could deny the effect the move had had a couple of nights earlier.

When Mack and Makayla first got put together, they had barely said two words to each other. But the ankle tie taught them to communicate and work together, and it did the job *fast*. Which, everyone agreed, was the name of the game at this point, on and off the basketball court.

The shouting died down as the players awkwardly shuffled along the steam-table line, trying to load up hamburgers with limited mobility and range of motion. Was it even fair to tease a team so desperate to improve that they'd commit to something like this?

Then Cassie stood up. "Hey, Pat," she yelled, "you want to join the basketball team?"

"CASSIE!" Nelson shrieked, slapping a hand over his eyes as the room broke into appreciative laughter. Even the players broke up this time, and Makayla, Nelson's three-legged buddy, patted him consolingly on the shoulder.

"What?!" Cassie shouted. "It looks like *fun!*"

For once in his life, Pat was speechless. Then he too stood up.

"You just want to get at my silver dollar!"

The camp groaned, and Cassie pretended to be hurt by the accusation.

Finally, the basketball players finished filling their trays and proceeded to the tables their fellow campers had cleared for them. Mack noticed they were already moving more naturally, walking in step with their partners.

He and Shona sat down at the nearest table, and Makayla and Nelson claimed the spots next to them. Then Cassie slid onto half of her brother's chair as usual.

As Mack raised his burger to his mouth, he heard Cassie whisper something worthy of printing on a T-shirt.

"This camp is crazy," she told Nelson. "I don't ever want to leave."

CHAPTER
23

"EVERYBODY OFF"

Over the next two days, three-legged walking became as natural to the basketball players as breathing. Brian and Tamara didn't even have to ask if they wanted to continue with Mack's plan—Miles simply kept track of the ankle ties and created new duos each morning and afternoon. The only times the players were consistently untethered were when they were practicing, sleeping, or using the bathroom.

Mack didn't want to toot his own horn—"Smart," Pat joked in their cabin one night, "because if you do, someone might try to break it over your head"—but the ploy immediately translated into results on the court. No, playing the fastest and most frenetic style of basketball ever invented wasn't much like walking around a summer camp, but the players all felt they were developing a sixth sense for one another's movements.

Just as they learned to predict when their partner was about to take a step or sneeze or turn around, they could suddenly tell when those same kids were going to back-cut their defenders or take off a second early to start a fast break.

During practice, they ran drill after drill to improve their cohesion on offense and defense, their recognition of which shots to take and which to pass up, and their ability to switch screens and trap opposing ball handlers. But it was their new and uncanny gift for anticipating each other's moves that awed their coaches.

And they owed it all to ankle ties.

So it was that on the first day of the Swish City 5-on-5, the junior-camp basketball players arrived at the bus two by two, each random pair walking in lockstep by force of habit.

The doors opened, and the players and coaches began to stream on. Mack, Miles, Andre, Nicole, and Makayla found seats halfway down the bus, but Wi-Fi peeled off and chose a seat near the front to ease his carsickness—the short trip to the fun zone had tested his limits, and he wasn't interested in losing his breakfast so close to the start of the tournament. He pulled a paper bag out of his backpack for emergency purposes, laid it flat on his lap, and looked up to find a familiar face.

"Pat?" he asked as his cabinmate climbed the stairs and passed him in the aisle. "What are you doing here?"

Pat shrugged. "I'm the mascot."

Then Wi-Fi noticed his old counselor climbing on as well.

"Laker?"

"I'm with Pat," he deadpanned.

Winston climbed up next. He'd been missing in action since storming out of the field house a few days earlier. No one knew where he'd been eating—or *if* he'd been eating—but they all knew he hadn't been showing up at the mess hall at mealtimes. Even now, his narrowed eyes and bulging jawbone told anyone paying attention that he hadn't got over his campers' mutiny.

"I'm sorry, fellas," he said to Pat and Laker, not sounding sorry at all. "I know you want to go to the tournament, but we can't take everyone."

Halfway down the bus, Miles poked his head over the seat in front of him and held up a clipboard. Already the team's unofficial statistician, he had taken on an official role as team manager, meaning he kept an eye on all the details. "They're on the list!" he said.

Winston pulled an identical clipboard from under his arm and flipped through its crisp white pages. "Half the camp is on this list!" he whined. "Nelson's little sister is on this list. It says she's co-manager!"

"To be fair," Cassie shouted from the back of the bus, "I'm on *every* list."

"And what's this about a cheering section?"

"That would be …" said Spike, sitting next to his twin.

"… us," finished Special K, crammed onto the seat with them.

Each of the three boys was wearing a loud tie-dyed T-shirt and had his face painted with a big black *C* on one cheek and orange *A* on the other.

Winston flopped onto a seat across from Wi-Fi. "They're going to laugh us out of the building," he muttered.

The driver cranked the key in the ignition, and the bus roared to life. As they pulled away from the office, Mack heard Cheryl's voice ring out over the camp loudspeakers: "Good luck to our junior-camp basketball team, just leaving for the Swish City tournament! We're all behind you!"

Thirty minutes of driving later—back roads giving way to city streets—the bus pulled up to a curb at the end of a row of other buses and smaller vans, next to what appeared to be a wide concrete wall.

Pat leaned over Mack and Miles to look out the window. "Uh, where's the gym?" he asked.

"Look up," Winston said, stifling a grin.

Pat and everyone else on the right side of the bus contorted themselves to look up at giant white letters that read "McGuire Sportsplex."

What they had parked beside was no random wall. It was a single pillar in a massive modern coliseum.

Nelson gulped. "We're playing in *there*?"

The bus doors opened, and Winston shouted, "Time to go! Everybody off."

Once outside, the kids grabbed their backpacks from the cargo holds beneath the bus and lined up so Miles and Cassie could do a head count. Then, like excited but frightened explorers, they set out along the subtle curve of the imposing building, straining their eyes in vain to see where it ended.

"I didn't notice before, but Cheryl put a Sportsplex fact sheet in here," Miles said, his eyes darting up and down a page buried deep in his clipboard. "This place is 135,000 square feet. There are sixteen volleyball courts, eight indoor hockey fields—"

Pat grabbed the clipboard. "There's a 400-meter track in there!" he gasped. "With pole vault and long jump pits and everything!"

"How many basketball courts?" Nicole asked, chiming in.

"Eight," Miles said. "With pristine glass backboards and ten-foot-wide computer-run scoreboards and seating for two thousand people."

Mack shuddered. The field house bleachers held maybe

two hundred. Suddenly their three-person cheering section felt incredibly modest.

"Well," Andre said, gaining his bearings, "we don't play on eight courts. We play on one."

"Exactly," Makayla agreed. "I've played in some big places."

"Not as big as this, maybe," Nicole said.

"No, but it's the same thing. It's just basketball."

After what felt like a long time, the Camp Average group reached its destination. The main doors sat at the base of a humongous glass wall that looked in on a cavernous registration area, which was festooned with giant blue-and-white Swish City banners.

A giant black hockey bag slung over his shoulder, Winston ushered the team inside. Seemingly every other team was already there, and Mack couldn't help but size up the competition. The boys and girls they'd be facing off against looked tall and chiseled, and they were decked out in shiny warm-up suits in every color of the rainbow. They had serious looks on their faces and chunky headphones on their ears.

Mack looked at his own teammates, a veritable bastion of unkempt hair and dirty fingernails. Their clothes were wrinkled and faded, and their high-tops all showed the scuff marks of being worn indoors and out.

We look like campers, he thought, *and everyone else looks like basketball players.*

"Okay," Winston said, nodding at the coaches, "I'll get us signed in."

He lifted his head and crossed the foyer, lugging his hockey bag behind him. Unlike his players, he was dressed to impress in a fresh-out-of-the-box black tracksuit. He'd even added lettering to the back of his jacket: "DIRECTOR" in big white capitals.

Winston joined the line of people waiting for their turn with a tournament official seated at a folding table. Then he spun in place—smiling confidently at the others in the room—to find Mack, Wi-Fi, and Miles standing right behind him.

Winston opened his mouth, likely to order them back to the rest of the group with a few stern words, but Mack stopped him by looking up with a wide smile.

The camp director frowned, then shrugged and smiled back.

Soon they'd reached the front of the line.

"Next!" the official shouted without looking up.

Winston pulled his shoulders back as he strode purposefully to the table. "Winston Smith from Camp Avalon," he boomed. "Here to sign in for the tournament."

The man behind the folding table nodded. "Sure

thing." He began mumbling to himself as he scrolled up and down a document on his laptop. "Camp Avalon, Camp Avalon ..." He frowned. "I'm afraid there's no registration for a Camp Avalon here. I just see a Camp *Average*, and you're not listed on it."

The man continued to stare at the screen while waiting for a response. Finally, he looked up at Winston, who was stone-faced, showing no emotion whatsoever.

"Sorry ... ?" Winston croaked.

"Camp Average," the man repeated, consolingly. "I know, kind of an odd name."

Still unmoving, Winston said, "There must be some mistake ..."

But Mack, Miles, and Wi-Fi cut around him and formed a barrier between their camp director and the table.

"That's us," Mack told the official.

The blood rushed back into Winston's face all at once, and he turned as red as his signature short shorts.

"I didn't pay for that entry!" he seethed.

"No, our parents did," Miles interjected meekly, buying Mack time to complete their registration. "We emailed them, and they were happy to do it. Camp Average has given us so much."

"But ... but what happened to the other entry? The one for Camp Avalon?"

"This *is* that entry," Wi-Fi offered just as quietly. "Cheryl changed the name."

"Cheryl?!"

Mack turned around. "Of course," he said, trying to remain calm in the face of Winston's anger. "Cheryl's got all the contacts. Basketball tournament organizers, exterminators, pool-repair companies ... lake-water cleaners."

Winston wilted. His shoulders slumped, and he took a step back.

"You know," Mack continued, "the pond by my house has the itch, and my dad has talked about raising some money to get it cleaned up. I should ask Cheryl who she called for our waterfront."

The camp director retreated another step as Mack's voice began picking up volume.

Uninterested until now, the others in the room—a mix of athletes, coaches, parents, and organizers—turned their heads to the source of the commotion as all other noise ceased at once. Winston saw them looking and shrank a little further.

"Or maybe you called the lake cleaners yourself?" Mack continued. "Either way, there'd be a record of it."

Mack knew this would make no sense to those listening in, but he didn't need them to understand.

"And if there isn't a record, that would mean one of only two things: either the beach should still be closed"— he paused—"or you *lied* to a bunch of kids about the whole thing."

Looking gray and deflated, Winston said nothing. He couldn't explain himself—not to Mack or anyone else— so he simply continued backing away as if being pulled off by an oversized hook in a TV talent show. Soon he'd backed all the way into the room's big glass double doors. Mack stopped five feet from him, watching his face and waiting for his next move. For a moment the camp director held his gaze, no hint of anger or determination left in his eyes. Only defeat.

Then he spun, shoved open the door, and bolted through it, leaning forward to compensate for the weight of his hockey bag. He crossed the massive parking lot at a sprint, never turning back.

Mack watched him until his far-off form disappeared entirely, then turned to his teammates. They mobbed him, shouting and cheering, as the other kids and adults in the foyer shrugged and went back to their business.

"Guys!" Mack shouted from the center of the fray. "We haven't won anything yet."

Andre put him in a loose headlock. "Not true, man," he said.

When the cheering finally died down, Mack heard another raised voice.

"Sir!" shouted the man behind the registration desk. "You haven't finished signing in!"

Mack reddened, running back to the table.

"Team name?" asked the man impatiently. "I just have an organization name here."

Mack furrowed his brow. They didn't have a mascot, unless you counted Pat. They didn't have a team name other than Camp Average. To Mack's mind, they weren't eagles or tigers or sharks. They were just who they were—kids who wanted to shoot baskets or water ski or do rocketry ...

Then his eyes lit up. "One more second," he said to the official.

He huddled up with his nineteen teammates, their arms instinctively wrapping around each other's shoulders. From the group came a unanimous shout: "Aye!"

Mack rushed back to the table a final time, nodding apologetically at the others in line. "For one weekend only," he declared, "we're the Rockets."

A whoop went up from the rest of the team, and Andre and Nicole enveloped Miles in a hug.

"Fine," said the frazzled official, typing furiously into his computer. "You're the Rockets."

Then he handed Mack a yellow welcome pack and a schedule printout.

"There are sixteen teams in the twelve-and-under bracket. Win four games and you win the tournament. Oh, and one more thing," he added. "You're playing in thirty minutes."

Mack's eyes went wide.

"Next!" the man shouted.

CHAPTER 24

"IT'S WORKING!"

Brian and Tamara led their players to the changerooms and ushered them inside. The coaches, managers, and cheerers stood in the hallway for only a minute before Mack popped his head back out.

"Um," he said, "the guys nominated me to ask what we're doing in here. We're already in our … uniforms."

Brian covered his face with both hands. "The hockey bag," he muttered.

They'd spent so much time working on their game, they hadn't put any thought into what they'd wear while playing. That had been the camp director's department, and he was probably halfway back to camp by now—with their jerseys and shorts slung over his shoulder.

Andre's head joined Mack's in the doorway. "Any intel?" he asked. And the problem became even clearer: the two best friends weren't even wearing the same color shirt.

Cassie scoffed at the coaches' stricken faces. "I guess

I *do* have to do everything myself," she huffed. She cracked open the door to the girls' changeroom. "Get out here!" she shouted. Then to the boys: "You, too."

The twenty players assembled in front of her, bags in hand. All ten girls were wearing orange T-shirts. Of the boys, three were wearing orange, six were wearing white, and one—Dillon—was wearing a black shirt with a skull on it.

"Dillon!" she admonished. "Where's your Camp Average gear?"

"It's all ripped!"

"Okay, who brought backup camp shirts? Pull them out," Cassie ordered.

All six of the boys in white pulled out orange shirts, and eight of the girls pulled out white. Special K, Spike, and Mike were wearing their cheering-section tie-dye. Pat was wearing white and said he was willing to trade.

"For a price," he added ominously.

That just left Mack, already wearing an orange shirt, digging frantically in his bag.

"We've got fifteen white shirts and nineteen orange so far," Nicole said.

"Mack, tell me you brought an extra orange," Cassie pleaded.

Mack knelt and dug into his bag, finally settling on

something. He dramatically pulled out a bright orange shirt. "I aim to please," he said.

Cassie sighed with relief. "Okay, then, we're in orange. Mack, give that shirt to Dillon."

"Fine," he said, tossing the shirt to his teammate. "But what do I wear between games?"

"Dillon, you got an extra skull shirt?"

Dillon pulled a black T-shirt out of his backpack. "Zombies," he said apologetically. "With, like, swords for hands."

"Good enough!" Cassie said. "Give that to Mack." She checked the clock. "The rest of you in white, change … *fast*. We've got fifteen minutes before game time, which gives me just enough time for the final touch."

She turned Nelson away from her, unzipped his backpack, and rummaged around until her hand settled on a black Sharpie.

"Perfect!" she said, then hastily began scrawling numbers on the players' backs.

Fittingly, Mack thought, he got number two.

He shook his head as Cassie moved on to other players, picking up a roll of black electrical tape that had spilled out of Nelson's bag. "Why exactly are you carrying this around?"

Nelson blushed, then reached into his backpack for the

Magic 8 Ball, which was taped around the center where it had cracked open.

"Nelson!"

"It works if you turn it upside down." He demonstrated by holding it above his head to look at the window on the underside, the die rattling into place. Mack, Wi-Fi, and Pat ducked under to read: "Outlook not so good."

"Well, at least that's not ominous or anything," Pat mumbled as Nelson tucked the ball back into his bag.

"I've got to say, Cassie was pretty impressive," Wi-Fi said, abruptly changing the subject. "All that problem-solving and there's basically no risk of any of us getting kicked out of camp. No offense, Mack."

"None taken," Mack replied, grinning.

Nelson nodded. "You should see her direct an unboxing video. You'd think it was a Hollywood blockbuster."

"The job isn't over yet, you know," said Cassie, over-hearing. "We're still a team called the Camp Average Rockets wearing T-shirts that say 'Camp Avalon.' I'll need to fix that for tomorrow."

Nelson shrugged. "We don't even know we're going to be playing tomorrow."

She looked her brother in the eye, seemingly trying to transmit some of her unshakeable confidence. "I do," she said curtly.

With ten minutes left before game time, the team finally walked through the doors of a gargantuan gymnasium. They found its gleaming, freshly waxed floor sectioned into four quadrants, each with its own basketball court and set of bleachers.

The players split the warm-up between a layup line and a passing drill on their half of their assigned court, then retreated to their benches—there were too many of them to fit on just one—when the buzzer sounded.

"Okay, you all know the drill," Brian told them, laying out the team's lineup chart in front of him:

	LINE 1	LINE 2	LINE 3	LINE 4
POINT GUARD	WI-FI	NICOLE	ELIJAH	BEA
SHOOTING GUARD	ELENA	GAVIN	KRISTI	NELSON
SMALL FORWARD	OMAR	DIANA	ANA	ANDRE
POWER FORWARD	JEWELL	DARNELL	LUIS	MIA
CENTER	MACK	SHONA	MAKAYLA	DILLON

"You know your lines and you know your rotations," Brian said. "When it's your turn to play, be ready."

Then he shot a glance over his shoulder at the opposing team, identified on the tournament schedule simply as

Beast. Mack counted eleven players—all thick, muscled boys who could've doubled as professional wrestlers.

"These guys will probably be better practiced than us," Brian continued. "They'll have played together longer than we have. They'll be—"

"Some people say it's sports we're worst at," interjected Pat, who'd snuck down from the stands to stand directly behind the coach, "but really it's pep talks."

"Pat?!" Brian jumped. "What are you even doing here?"

"I'm the mascot!" Pat said incredulously. "I'm doing *my job*. But I guess I can give you a minute."

"Give us, like, two days," Andre chided, drawing a tension-breaking laugh from his team.

Pat narrowed his eyes, then slunk back to the stands.

"As Brian was saying," Tamara picked up the thread, "they might be a lot of things we're not. But they've never seen anything like us."

"*Nobody* has," Brian added. "Bring it in."

All twenty players bounced off the bench and formed a scrum, pushing their hands into the middle.

"One, two, three …"

"AVERAGE!"

The lines had been split up so Mack, Andre, Nicole, and Makayla each anchored one, and they'd all determined that Mack's should begin the game—

when he was actually trying, he was the best at taking tip-offs.

He slapped several hands and took the court with Wi-Fi, Elena, Omar, and Jewell, their black-marker numbers crooked and slightly smeared on their backs.

"Well," Pat said to Laker in the stands, "at least no one will overestimate us based on style."

Mack stepped to the center circle, shook hands with the boy opposite him—he was maybe an inch shorter, but far thicker in the arms and shoulders—and crouched, ready to leap. The ref checked his watch quickly, then immediately threw the ball up into the air.

Mack and the other center leapt like cats and tapped the ball simultaneously. It squirted up and back toward the Beast side of the floor, landing in the hands of the team's point guard.

"Get back on defense!" yelled Tamara.

But as the Camp Average players scrambled to find their checks, the ball pinged between Beast players and wound up with their wide-open small forward. He put up a smooth-looking jump shot, and it fell through the net.

Ten seconds into the game, it was 2–0 Beast.

"Shake it off!" shouted Brian.

Mack grabbed the ball and passed it inbounds to Wi-Fi, then the pair charged up the floor at top speed.

They had only about three and a half more minutes in their shift—why waste time by walking it up?

Wi-Fi yelled out, "One!" and held a finger up in the air, now both a sarcastic nod at Winston and a new running joke. In reality, they had only one play, and it was really more of a strategy—just pass and move until someone gets a great look at the hoop.

Wi-Fi whipped the ball to Omar on the left wing, then sprinted for the far corner of the court. Meanwhile, Mack—on the left low block—set a screen under the hoop for Jewell, who burst free.

"Jewell's open!" Brian shouted.

But by the time the coach had opened his mouth, the ball was already in the air, flitting off Omar's fingers toward its target. Jewell caught it under the basket and put up a left-handed hook shot … but rushed it.

The ball hit the backboard and bounced harmlessly off the rim, falling into the hands of a waiting defender.

"Outlet!" shouted the Beast point guard, calling for the ball. He caught a pass and took off. When he reached the top of the key, he maintained his dribble and scanned the court.

Clinging close to her check on the wing, Jewell clapped her hands in frustration. "I should've had that," she seethed.

"Just be ready for the next one!" Mack encouraged her from the low post. "Could come along *soon*."

Jewell's eyes narrowed in recognition. From the opposite wing, Omar charged the ball handler with his hands high in the air, cutting off a pass. Reflexively, the point guard spun-dribbled away from him, but he quickly realized his mistake. Before his body had even performed the full rotation, Jewell materialized on his blind side to steal the ball. Then she kept her momentum and sprinted up the court. When she banked in the first two Camp Average points of the game, she was a full twenty feet ahead of the next closest Beast player.

"Yes!" Wi-Fi pumped his fist.

Jewell pointed back at Omar. "All you!" she shouted.

As the Beast center and point guard jogged toward their net to inbound the ball, they glanced suspiciously at Jewell, who hadn't moved an inch from her spot under the hoop.

The center picked the ball off the floor and crossed the baseline out of bounds. He whirled and found Jewell in his face, jumping and waving her arms. He could barely see past her, but what he saw was unnerving: Mack was blanketing his point guard.

"Move!" the center shouted to his teammate, knowing he had only five seconds to get the ball inbounds.

"I'm trying!" the point guard returned, frantically trying to break free.

The center tried lobbing the ball over Mack's head, but the plan failed. Mack jumped and pulled the ball out of the air. Then he took one dribble and laid it in off the glass backboard.

The Beast center shouted "Come on!" to himself, then grabbed the ball for a second attempt. This time, he found Mack blocking his view and Jewell draped all over his point guard.

"Help!" he yelled, beckoning his teammates to come back.

But it was too late.

TWEET!

"Five-second violation," the ref said. "Rockets' ball."

As the Beast players hung their heads, the Rockets who'd been guarding them barreled down the court. So when the ref handed Mack the ball, Jewell simply had to clear out to the three-point line to leave a wide-open lane for Wi-Fi to run down. He caught a pass from Mack, took two steps without dribbling, and flipped the ball expertly into the hoop.

The now-fuming Beast center again grabbed the ball and finally inbounded it to an open man—the team's power forward—before the Camp Average players could recover.

Then they recovered.

Omar and Jewell both sprinted to the ball handler, trapping him on the sideline. Unaccustomed to this much pressure, the power forward tried to force the ball back to his point guard. But Wi-Fi stepped into the passing lane. He caught the ball and redirected it to Elena as if setting a volleyball. She caught it at the free-throw line and nailed a short jump shot.

"It's working!" Cassie shouted from the bench. Then she put her mouth to her brother's ear before he could squirm away. "IT'S WORRRRRKIIIIING!"

Eight unanswered points, and suddenly Camp Average was up by six.

"Time out!" shouted the Beast coach.

Mack and the rest of his line returned to the bench, high-fiving each other the whole way.

"Awesome job, you guys," said Brian, handing out water bottles as the heavy-breathing group flopped down onto the bench. "That's *exactly* how we want to play. Fast, hard, unselfish."

"When you set those traps," Tamara chimed in, "keep talking and rotating to the closest open man. They'll get better at recognizing it, but they won't be able to keep up."

Brian checked the game clock. "Speaking of which,

we've got fresh legs coming in." He looked down his long line of players. "Nicole's line, you're on."

Wi-Fi's eyes bugged out. "That was four minutes already?"

"It's gonna go fast when you're playing that hard," Tamara said.

Still gasping for air, Mack put out a fist for Nicole to bump. "Go get 'em," he croaked.

"You know we will," she replied.

CHAPTER
25

"I LIKE IT"

The Beast players returning to the court looked relieved as the new line came on—maybe this five wouldn't be as energetic—but they quickly realized they were in for more of the same. Nicole hounded the inbounder into throwing the ball out of bounds, then hit the game's first three-pointer a few seconds later.

On the bench, Mack chugged water from his bottle. He'd chosen the seat next to Miles, who was updating a spreadsheet on a laptop he'd borrowed from Cheryl.

Mack watched him mark both a three-point attempt and a make for Nicole, and an assist for Darnell. The spreadsheet then auto-populated cells for Nicole's field-goal and three-point percentages.

"Rockets, eh?" Miles said, his eyes darting between the court and the computer.

"You know it."

"I like it." The manager grinned.

On the court, the Beast players successfully inbounded the ball to their point guard, which drew a thankful cheer from their bench. Mack and Miles watched as Gavin got in front of the ball handler, staying low, sliding his feet, and funneling him toward the sideline. The point guard tried to beat Gavin to a narrow corridor of court between them and the sideline, but he stepped out of bounds.

Mack jumped up. "Yeah!" he shouted, clapping. Then he dragged Nelson to his feet, and the other thirteen players on the bench followed suit. Suddenly, it was a standing ovation.

"Let's GO!" shouted Andre.

Mack looked up into the stands as his teammates flew around the court, inbounding the ball with ease and leaving the Beast players in their dust as they passed and moved, passed and moved. He saw the amazed looks on the faces of the spectators as they puzzled out the same question: Who were these players dressed in dirty laundry and treating basketball like it was a track meet?

Even as the Beast coaches helped their charges figure out how to consistently get the ball in play and over half court after Camp Average scored, Makayla's and Andre's lines kept the pressure on and the points coming. And when the Beast players crowded the area around the hoop to eliminate layup opportunities, Camp Average adjusted by taking more wide-open long-range shots.

Playing on Andre's line, Nelson sank three of his five three-point attempts. He could've done even more damage, but he froze up and turned the ball over twice as defenders started covering him more closely.

At the half, it was 32–14.

By the time the third quarter started, the Beast players had settled down enough to start getting the kinds of shots they wanted. One player in particular, a tall guard with a lightning-quick jump shot release, scored baskets on three consecutive possessions.

Inbounding the ball after the third bucket, Mack had to admit the guard was good. But he was also gasping for air.

Mack and his linemates poured on the pressure, knowing their time on the court was quickly running out, while their opponents slowed down more and more. And despite the early-period Beast surge, the shift ended with Camp Average up 42–24.

Once more on the bench, Mack realized this was the final brilliant element of their plan. Opposing teams had to choose—play the kids they usually did and watch them tire out over the course of the game, or sit them for longer stretches in favor of players who didn't get as much court time and might not be as prepared.

This wasn't an insurmountable problem if you had some time to work it out—just as the Camp Average players had done with a few days' practice—but in the midst of a game, there was no good option.

So as the clock ticked down in the fourth quarter, the gap between the two teams only increased. Even with Andre's line's sportsmanlike attempts to not run up the score, the contest still ended with a lopsided 68–36 tally.

As the final buzzer sounded, the Camp Average cheering section went nuts.

"We …" said Spike.

"… did …" added Mike.

"… it!" finished Special K.

The actual team's response was surprisingly subdued. Andre's line sprinted to the sideline for a quick round of fist bumps, then together all four lines headed to the other team's bench to shake hands with their dejected opponents.

The players grabbed their bags and water bottles, then met up with their cheerleaders and "mascot" in the shadow of the bleachers for a quick huddle and debrief.

"Great job, you guys," Tamara said, beaming. "We couldn't be prouder of what you did out there."

"I guess now's a good time to tell you," Brian added. "That team you just beat? They've lost twice all summer—in about thirty games. I asked around in the foyer earlier, and most people thought they'd reach the final."

The Camp Average players were dumbfounded.

"They ... *what*?" Makayla asked.

Miles unfolded the tournament program from their yellow welcome packet and held it out for all to see. It had a picture of a Beast player on the cover.

"I didn't want to tell you before, but Beast is the featured team in here," Miles said. "There's a two-page write-up on them. The guy who went on that run in the third quarter has been averaging about forty points per game."

"How many did he score against us?" asked Nelson.

"Fourteen."

The Camp Average players' eyes darted around, assessing each other, the stands, the ceiling. The entire gleaming, enormous room.

Maybe they belonged there after all. If they could knock off the tournament favorite—by thirty-two points, no less—what else were they capable of?

CHAPTER 26

"TRUST YOUR GUT!"

With ninety minutes between games, the team hunkered down in a quiet hallway to eat sub sandwiches and study the tournament bracket. Miles had pulled the poster-sized version of it from the middle of the program and laid it flat on the floor.

"Beating Beast puts us into the Elite Eight—"

"Wait, we're already 'elite'?" Andre asked.

"I guess so," Miles replied, "but really that's just what they call it in big basketball tournaments. Like, Sweet Sixteen, Final Four ..."

"What's the name for the last two?" Pat asked.

"DICTIONARY!" called Mack, feeling strangely powerful in Dillon's zombie T-shirt.

Miles thought for a second. "They don't have one, I don't think," he said. "It's just called the final."

Pat stood up and saluted. "I'm on it."

"On what?" Mack asked.

"Mack, you don't need to twist my arm. I've got this."

Then Pat walked away mumbling to himself. "Terrific Two? No, too obvious. Terrible Two? Not exactly accurate."

Miles returned to the bracket. "We'll be playing a team called BC Select. They won their first-round game by five."

"Is that it?" Nicole grinned. "I bet they're terrified right now."

But if the Camp Average players thought their big win had earned them a little respect, they were quickly brought down to Earth when they reentered the gym.

As they ran their dual warm-up drills, a few of their opponents gathered at center court to watch them. The BC Select players were decked out in shiny short-sleeve tops and shorts, with fluorescent-yellow high-tops that made it look like they were sponsored by a sports-apparel company.

"Hey, check it, guys," said an athletic-looking girl with black neoprene sleeves on her arms and legs. "We're playing a daycare team."

"I like their uniforms," said a sneering boy with black face paint under each eye. "I have a beat-up punching bag at home that looks exactly like them."

"Gotta give it to their camp name, though." The girl cracked her knuckles. "They look ... average."

Standing ten feet away, whipping chest passes back and forth with Luis, Mack heard every word.

He also heard Pat, who was standing behind the Camp Average bench, arguing with Laker. "I just said I'd *show* him a punching bag! So let me onto the court, okay?"

Mack couldn't help but smile, but he was still tense and on high alert for anything personal from the gawkers at center court. He hated the way "average" sounded coming out of their mouths—it seemed like a dirty word.

He looked around at his teammates. Yes, some of the eleven-year-olds were smaller than many of the others at the tournament, and no, their uniforms weren't anything to write home about. But they were *his* teammates, and he wasn't about to let someone hurt them.

"Don't listen to them," Elena said from beside him, reading his body language. "They're jerks, for sure. But they also have no idea who they're dealing with. They wouldn't be standing there laughing if they did."

Mack thought about this.

"The only way someone's going to beat us is by taking us seriously," she continued. "And these guys *aren't*."

With a steely look of determination, Mack nodded. "You're exactly right," he said.

Soon he was standing again with one foot in the center circle, ready for the tip-off.

"I'd accuse you of buying a win in round one," the opposing center grunted, "but it doesn't look like you have the money."

Mack tried to channel his inner Pat to think up a comeback. But as the ref approached them, he simply met his rival's gaze.

"What?" The center scowled.

"It's 2–0."

The ref threw the ball up, and Mack leapt first. But he didn't tip it backward this time. Instead, he batted it—hard—into the front court. The ball shot toward the free-throw line and into the hands of a streaking Elena, who laid it into the hoop easily.

Four seconds into the game, 2–0.

By four minutes into the game, Mack's line had ballooned their lead to eight. Just as Elena had predicted, BC Select didn't know how to handle the speed and pressure that had become the Rockets' hallmarks.

As the first batch of Camp Average subs bounced onto the court, Mack grabbed his bottle and shot a stream of water into the back of his throat.

"Nice shift, Mack!" someone shouted from the stands.

Mack smiled. Then he furrowed his brow.

He didn't recognize the voice.

He swiveled in his seat and discovered a small boy in a

purple-and-yellow warm-up suit. Judging by his immaculately styled hair and unscuffed shoes, Mack guessed he was a benchwarmer on an eliminated team, and waved awkwardly.

The kid turned to two friends in matching warm-ups. "He waved at me!"

Mack noticed a few similar-looking groups hovering around Camp Average's own supporters—one group was even decked out in Beast gear. He also saw Pat bouncing between them, chatting them up.

"Guess that explains how they knew my name," he muttered.

Later, as the last shift of the half began, Mack noted that the gaps in the larger cheering section had filled, and that the section's biggest cheers were for Nelson, who had evidently been identified as the famous YouTube host.

In the final minute of the quarter, the crowd favorite hit a three-pointer off a pass from Mia, and his fans erupted.

"MVP! MVP!" one of them chanted.

Then he stole the ball and got another opportunity to increase their advantage before the buzzer, but this time he was blanketed by a defender.

With six seconds left on the clock, Nelson's indecision took hold.

"Dribble it!" someone in the stands yelled down at him.

"Shoot it!" yelled another.

"Pass it!" yelled Andre, standing on the wing with his hands up.

"TRUST YOUR GUT!" yelled Cassie, louder than them all.

Nelson jerked the ball from his hip to above his head to his shooting pocket and back to his hip again.

TWEET!

"Travel!" the ref yelled, rotating his fists one over the other in a wheel motion.

Nelson looked down at his feet, which had been scuffling along the floor as he cycled through his options. He scowled and shouted, "Sorry, guys!"

The BC Select players inbounded the ball, but the buzzer sounded before they could get off a desperation shot.

Score at the half: 30–14.

Still, Nelson steamed toward the bench, scolding himself under his breath as if they were down by twenty.

Mack intercepted him, trying to defuse the situation. "Hey, New Money, don't worry about it. It was just one—"

"Save it, Mack." Nelson hopped the bench to pick up his backpack. "I don't say this often, so trust me: I know what I gotta do."

For a split second, Mack worried that Nelson was going to walk out of the gym, but instead he thrust his hand inside the bag, searched around, and came up with a shiny black object. The Magic 8 Ball.

Oh, no, Mack thought, *this is worse.*

"Nelson, man, I don't think—"

But Nelson stopped him with a look that said, "I got this."

He walked over to the stands, which erupted in cheers. Then he pointed at a boy in the fourth row and tossed him the ball. First the boy raised it over his head in a triumphant pose, then he brought it low to examine it—a broken toy with tape wrapped around it.

"Shake it," Nelson told him.

The boy obliged, and the die rattled loudly inside the plastic orb. A perfect noisemaker.

The kids around him cheered, and Nelson walked back to the bench.

"Had to be done," he told Mack, flushing. "I knew it as soon as Cassie said it."

Mack raised a questioning eyebrow.

"Trust your gut," Nelson said.

During the second half, the Camp Average craze only got bigger. So when Andre and his linemates jogged the length of the bleachers to warm up before their fourth-quarter shift, the fans in their section did the wave in unison as they passed.

"This is crazy!" Andre shouted as he hopped past Mack, who simply nodded.

With few fouls and no time-outs during the final shift, the game was over in a flash.

Final score: 50–27.

The teams shook hands. Mack neared the sneering center he'd faced at tip-off, expecting a choked "Good game" or maybe a "Sorry." But he didn't get it.

"I doubt you'll make it to the finals," the center taunted. "But good luck if you do. You'll need it."

"What? Why?" Mack asked, blindsided.

"Because Roundrock," the center replied as he moved off in the other direction, "they play just like you."

CHAPTER
27

"WHAT CHOICE DO WE HAVE?"

After Mack told his teammates what he'd learned about Roundrock, they all boarded the bus and returned to camp in a state of somber exhaustion. So far, their playing style had been like scissors cutting paper, but what would happen if they met a sharper, more expensive pair of scissors?

The players sleepwalked through dinner and evening activities, barely registering their campmates' constant cheers and congratulations, and crashed at the earliest opportunity. They woke up early, ate breakfast as a unit, and assembled in front of the office at 8:00 a.m. on the dot, exactly two hours before tip-off of their semifinal game.

Despite their anxiety about facing off against Roundrock—if they even made it through the semis—they were a single-minded machine. Only one component was missing.

"Where's the bus?" Pat asked.

The team waited five minutes. Then ten.

The office door popped open, and Cheryl poked her head out. "Still nothing?"

The players shook their heads.

"I'm sure it's just … traffic."

She disappeared again, closing the door behind her.

Pat plumped his backpack into a cushion and sat down on it in the road. "Yeah, I hear traffic's brutal on Sunday mornings." He paused. "In the woods."

Cheryl reemerged a few moments later, beckoning the coaches to the front of the office. Their eyes widened as she whispered, and then Brian took off at a dead run down the hill.

When he returned, shaking his head at Cheryl and Tamara, Mack asked for an explanation.

Cheryl heaved a sigh. "The bus isn't coming."

"Why not?" Andre blinked. "Where is it?"

"Two hours away. It wasn't just cancelled without me knowing. It was sent for a fake pickup in the opposite direction."

"But who would—" Nicole started.

Mack clenched his jaw. "Winston," he said through his teeth.

"Yeah," Brian confirmed. "And he's nowhere to be

found. His cabin is empty. I'm guessing his wheels are gone, too."

The camp director—*former* camp director—had burned his last bridge on his way out, ensuring he'd never be allowed back. But Mack was too upset to celebrate.

Cheryl stepped forward hopefully. "We're not totally sunk yet, guys. A few of the counselors have cars here," she offered. "We can get seven or eight of you there with time to spare."

The players looked around at each other. How would they even begin figuring out who goes and who stays?

"No," Nicole spoke for the team. "That won't work."

"But we've still got an hour and forty minutes, and—" Cheryl began.

Mack breathed out his nose. "We appreciate it, but this isn't a principle thing."

"For once," Pat added.

"We just don't know how to play like an eight-person team. Our strength is literally in our numbers."

"We've lost," Nicole said. "It's over."

Andre stepped forward. "Maybe not," he said. "Or at least … not yet."

"What do you mean?" Brian asked.

"I know a place with its own buses," he said flatly, giving nothing away. "Cheryl, can I use your phone?"

Thirty minutes later, the assembled kids spotted a dirt cloud rising above the trees at the mouth of their driveway and knew their ride had arrived. When the bus descended the final stretch of road into camp, they saw it was dark blue with white lettering.

And the lettering said "Camp Killington."

"Andre?!" Mack shouted.

"What?" he shot back. "You got another idea?"

The bus stopped in front of the office. Its doors opened, and a face familiar to any camp baseball player emerged.

"You've gotta be kidding me," Mack mumbled.

"What's up, Average?" boomed Terry Dietrich, the star of the Killington team. "I hear you guys need a lift."

A cheer rose up from the group, and the basketball players poured on. There was only an hour left until tip-off, and they had no time to waste.

Still, Mack was reluctant. Guys like Deets didn't do favors for nothing. What would it mean when they accepted this ride?

Andre nudged him. "What choice do we have?"

As his friend climbed the bus steps, Mack reached for the grab bar inside the door, pausing for just a moment before following.

The two had barely dropped into their seats when the door slammed shut and the driver—a big man with a bushy black mustache and a name tag that read "Morgan"—pressed down on the accelerator. They were onto the main road before anyone spoke.

"So," Deets said, "my boy Jenner tells me you guys are in some sort of basketball tournament?"

"Who's Jenner?" Miles whispered to Mack.

"*Me*," Andre said. "It's short for Jennings."

"What?" Deets asked. "You prefer Dre?"

"He prefers Andre, *Terrence!*" Pat stood to confront Deets before being yanked back down to his seat by Laker.

The kids sat in silence for a few minutes. Then Deets abruptly picked up where he'd left off.

"Okay, Dre it is. Anyway, he told me you reached the semis. That's not bad. Think you can make the finals?"

"Of course we can make—" Nicole began before getting cut off by an urgent shout.

"Hang on to something, kids!"

The passengers clutched their seats while Morgan slammed on the brakes and pulled off to the side of the road. Mack looked out the window. They were stopped on a wide gravel shoulder next to a farmer's field just outside the city limits.

"Why are we stopped?" Nelson asked.

The players got their answer as Morgan cranked the key again and again, but the bus refused to start.

He went outside and opened the large front hood, only to return a few minutes later and remove his hat in a gesture of defeat.

"We're stuck," he said, drawing a groan from the group. "We've lost power to the fuel injectors. Bus can't run like that."

After a moment, Wi-Fi, always in the mood to talk technical issues, asked, "What caused it?"

"Just time," Morgan said. "There's a little clip that holds one harness to another. After a while, it loosens up and they separate."

"So you need a new part," Wi-Fi said. "But is there any way to fix it temporarily?"

The driver squinted and scratched his forehead. "Give me a second."

He pulled a smartphone out of his pocket and made a call, everyone on the bus watching his every muscle spasm. He talked for all of sixty seconds before hanging up.

Then he turned with a hopeful look on his face. "Anybody got a quarter?"

The hope that had built during the call was suddenly dashed as the kids shook their heads in unison. They were carrying basically what they had on their backs. None of them had any money at all.

Mack shot a pleading look at their coaches.

"Sorry," Brian said, looking sick. "We don't even get paid until the end of summer."

Finally, he cast his eyes on Deets, who was leaning over the seat in front of him.

"Not me, man. I only carry cards."

Morgan scanned their dejected faces. "My guy told me a quarter could do the job, but I'm willing to try *any* coin. A nickel or a British pound"—he was patting his pockets and grasping at straws—"or a silver dollar ..."

The barely audible words boomed the entire length of the bus. All eyes turned to Pat, alone in a seat near the back. Somehow even Deets knew to look in his direction.

"What?" Pat asked.

"A silver dollar!" Mack shouted. "*You've* got a silver dollar!"

Pat's face was blank. "Says who?"

"Says *you*! You never stop talking about it!"

Again, Pat didn't react. "Doesn't sound like me."

As the passengers shouted and threw up their hands in frustration, Mack quietly slid into the seat next to Pat. He planted a hand on his friend's shoulder. "It's the only way, man," he soothed. "You know I wouldn't ask if it wasn't."

Pat stared at the seat in front of him. "You know I wouldn't give it if that wasn't a double negative," he mocked, weakly.

"*Pat*," Mack pleaded.

"Okay, *fine*," he growled. "Move!"

Mack stood, and Pat ducked his head under the seat. Then he yanked his shoe and sock off, revealing a layer of duct tape around his foot.

"So *that's* why you've been showering in beach shoes all summer!" Mack exclaimed.

"Well," Pat said, "this and floor germs."

He peeled the tape to reveal the infamous silver dollar in a clear plastic baggie. Then he tipped the coin out and looked away as he gave it to Mack.

"Go quick before I change my mind."

Kids dove out of Mack's way as he ran up the aisle to pass the dollar to Morgan.

"This'll do," the driver said, appraising it.

He descended the stairs in a single leap, bolted to the open hood, and carefully stuck the coin in place. "Try it!" he shouted, wiping grease from his hands with a rag.

Tamara leapt to the driver's seat and cranked the key in the ignition, and the bus fired to life.

The kids inside the bus chanted, "Pa-at, Pa-at, Pa-at!" But the man of the hour was too distraught to enjoy the attention. He covered his face with one hand and waved everyone away with the other.

"*Man*, you guys are weird," Deets muttered.

Cassie stood from her seat, pointing a finger in his face. "And don't you forget it!"

Fifteen minutes later, the bus screamed into the sportsplex parking lot.

"Okay, you players on the first line," Brian bellowed. "The run to the court *is* your warm-up. We don't have time for anything else. So make it count."

The bus screeched to a stop at exactly 9:59—one minute until game time—and the kids poured off, raining heartfelt thank-yous on Morgan as they went.

Having spent the remainder of the ride stretching out his arms and legs in the bus aisle, Mack led his line through the large glass doors, down the hall, and into the gym, where they were met first with gasps and then with cheers. The starting five for their opponents—a co-ed team in maroon uniforms with white lettering, known in the program as Triple Threat Youth—were already waiting impatiently at center court.

The Camp Average starters ditched their bags, wiped the bottoms of their shoes with their hands, and bolted onto the court.

From that point on, the game was a blur—in Mack's eyes, anyway. Triple Threat quickly jumped out to a 6–0 lead, but once he and his linemates got their legs under them, they converted three straight layups to knot the score. Then the other lines picked up right where they left off, and the lead increased thanks to a hail of swishes on one end and swatted shots on the other.

Nobody on the team would ever say it, but after the seemingly impossible feat of just getting to the gym, the game seemed easy. At the end of four furiously paced quarters, Camp Average had won again: 58–35.

The players shook hands with their opponents and returned to the bench. Only then did things slow down long enough for them to take in the enormity of the moment.

They had just made the finals.

CHAPTER
28

"WHO'S PUMPED UP?!"

The team hunkered down in the hallway outside the gym, awed by the dawning reality. "Congratulations," Pat said dramatically, walking amongst the group, "on making the *Tremendous* Two."

The players stared at him for a second and then realized: he was unveiling his name for the final.

"What about 'amazing'?" asked Gavin after a few seconds. "As in, the Amazing Two?"

Pat gritted his teeth. "It doesn't start with *T*. There's no alliteration!"

Other teammates chimed in with a flurry of questions.

"What about 'top'?"

"What about 'talented'?"

"What's alliteration?"

"No, no, and *ask Miles*! It's 'tremendous'! We're going with 'tremendous'!" Pat closed his eyes and sucked air through his teeth. "I lost my silver dollar today. Just give me this."

Mack put an arm around him. "You got it, buddy. 'Tremendous' it is." He nodded encouragingly at his teammates.

"I for one really like it," Miles jumped in. To the rest of the group, he whispered, "Alliteration is when consecutive words start with the same letter sound. Like 'Final Four.'"

"Or 'Tremendous Two'!" Pat wailed as Mack walked him away.

The twelve-and-under tournament final was at one o'clock, but the minutes between games disappeared like cheeseburgers in the Camp Average mess hall on BBQ night. Before the players knew it, they had finished their warm-up and were back on the court for team introductions.

"Welcome, one and all, to the twelve-and-under final of the Swish City 5-on-5," a tall woman in a gray suit said into a microphone at center court. The stands were full now, and Mack saw several men and women dressed like Laker's brother at their grudge match back at camp. But these might have been real scouts. "I'm Candace Burke, the tournament director, and I have the distinct pleasure of introducing you to our teams, Camp Roundrock and Camp ... er, Average!"

The two teams were lined up facing the crowd on either side of Candace, who started with Roundrock.

Mack stole the opportunity to fully size up the competition—and immediately wished he hadn't. The sight made his stomach do somersaults.

The players, when taken together, looked like a professional team. Their tight-fitting blue-and-red uniforms were only part of the picture. Given their consistent size, Mack couldn't tell by looking at them who played which position. Or maybe they were beyond specific roles because they were just that good.

"And finally, last year's tournament MVP, Samar Singh!" Candace shouted.

The player closest to her gave a quick wave to the crowd, then dapped fists with the player next to him. He was long-armed and broad-shouldered and wore a red turban on his head.

"They call him *Slam*ar," Andre whispered in Mack's ear. "I hear he can already dunk a volleyball."

Mack thought for a second. "Pat really needs to work on our intimidating nicknames," he mused.

Andre giggled. "'That's Mack,'" he said, putting on a nervous, excited voice. "'They call him that because … it's the first syllable in Mackenzie.'"

Then Candace moved on to the Camp Average introductions. The list was so long her voice started cracking halfway through and she had to take a sip of water.

"Okay, teams!" she shouted hoarsely when the job was finally done. "You've got two minutes. Then we'll be ready to determine our champion."

The players ran to their benches. Mack's line began hopping in place and stretching out their limbs. Then Brian and Tamara gathered everyone—managers and mascot and all—into a giant huddle.

"We were going to give a big speech," Tamara said, "but you guys know what you have to do. Roundrock may play like us, but they don't have our numbers. So just keep doing your thing. At the end of the day, you'll be proud of yourselves, no matter the outcome."

"Anybody else got anything they'd like to say?" Brian asked.

The players all instinctively looked at Mack.

"Really?" he said.

Andre pointed at his wrist. "Sixty seconds, man."

Mack dug into the recesses of his mind for something inspiring. Then he blurted, "I didn't even want to play on this team."

"Classic Mack pep talk!" Pat squeaked.

Mack tried to glare at his friend but couldn't. He grinned instead. "I wanted to go waterskiing."

"WHO'S PUMPED UP?!"

"But forget waterskiing. Forget everything I did and

didn't want to do this summer." He took a deep breath. "If I hadn't done this with all of you, I would've regretted it forever."

Mack felt Andre's arm squeeze around his neck as their teammates put their foreheads together for a team scream.

TWEET!

"Time to take the court, Average!" the ref shouted impatiently, ball in hand.

Mack high-fived each of his linemates, then stepped onto the court, squeaking his shoes against the freshly waxed floor. As he approached the dot, he could already imagine the snide remarks he'd get from Slamar, the opposing center, who was waiting there for him.

Maybe: "Thanks for finally showing up."

Or: "For Rockets, you guys sure are slow."

Or another dig at their uniforms: "What, you get stuck at the tailor?"

But as he looked at the floor to plant his foot by the centerline, a fist slowly hovered into view.

"Heard your bus broke down this morning," Slamar said when Mack looked up. "That sucks."

"Yeah," Mack agreed.

He thought this would be an awkward time to add, "Especially after our camp director deliberately sent the bus we should've caught into the next time zone, and then we had to make a deal with the Killington devil just to get here at all. Oh yeah, and we also lost a treasured silver dollar."

So instead, he lightly bumped Slamar's fist and said, "Thanks. Have a good game."

"You, too."

The ball went up, and the quick-leaping Slamar tipped it back to his point guard, who wasted no time pushing it up the court.

"Get back!" Mack shouted, and his team responded, recovering before Roundrock could get a bucket in transition.

The ball whipped around the court before settling back into the point guard's hands. He crossed the ball over, freezing Wi-Fi in his tracks, then blew by him to hit a floating jump shot in the lane.

Wi-Fi cursed himself as he caught an inbounds pass from Mack. But in his momentary anger, he forgot that Roundrock would be running a full-court press, too. When he turned to dribble up the court, the point guard stripped the ball and scored an easy layup.

"Gah!" Wi-Fi grunted.

Camp Average quickly figured out the press, carefully working the ball up the court with pinpoint passes. But as they settled into their half-court offense, they looked more like the two teams that had squared off in their first intra-camp grudge match than the one team they'd grown into by tournament time.

The ball pinged awkwardly back and forth around the perimeter, each pass taking the players farther away from the hoop. With three seconds left on the shot clock, Elena caught the ball on the wing. Mack pointed at the sky, imploring her to shoot, but instead she whipped a pass to him in the post, and the clock ran out before he could get a shot up.

"Let's go, guys!" Brian shouted from the sidelines. "Play your game!"

At the sound of Brian's voice, Wi-Fi's eyes popped open like he'd sniffed smelling salts. When he brushed past Mack on defense, he said, "Next half-court possession, screen left."

Seconds later, Jewell dove on a loose ball to get the first Camp Average stop of the game. She flipped the ball to Wi-Fi, who charged across center court and dribbled to a stop at the top of the three-point line, giving his team a chance to catch up. Mack set a screen to the left shoulder of Wi-Fi's defender. Then Wi-Fi dribbled hard around the screen, and Mack spun—or "rolled"—to follow him into the paint.

He had a sudden strong feeling of déjà vu. They hadn't run a lot of screen-and-rolls, so why did this feel so familiar?

Then he twigged.

No no no no no, he thought.

As they neared the hoop, Wi-Fi brought the ball behind his back in his right hand, bouncing it high off the floor to Mack.

Unlike the last time Wi-Fi had tried this maneuver, Mack was ready. He leapt high, caught the ball at the top of his jump, and put it off the glass for a layup.

"A behind-the-back bounce alley-oop pass!" Pat screamed from the stands, and the crowd went wild around him.

Mack grinned at Wi-Fi as they rushed to their checks.

"*Our* game!" Wi-Fi shouted.

That bucket gave way to a back-and-forth scoring binge, and each team notched six more points by the first Camp Average shift change.

"They're good," Mack said as he collapsed on the bench at the four-minute mark. "And we're"—he tracked his five teammates as they headed out onto the court—"wearing headbands?"

Nicole and the rest of the players on her line were sporting brand-new electric-orange headbands. On one side they read "Average" in black block letters, and on the other "Rockets."

Mack looked down the bench, and he saw that every player—save the ones on his line—was wearing one.

"What's with—" he started before Cassie tapped him

on the shoulder, lugging a cardboard box behind her. She reached in, grabbed a headband, and handed it to him.

"Fixing our whole lack-of-team-apparel problem," she told him. "A local screen printer does T-shirts for our YouTube channel, so he gave me a deal on these. Just needed a minimum order of two hundred."

Mack gasped. "Two hundred!"

"I thought about ordering full uniforms," Cassie charged ahead, casting aside Mack's protest, "but how am I supposed to know your sizes? Besides, now Pat has something to throw at random kids."

At just that moment, Pat was in the stands, facing away from the court, twirling a headband above him and stirring the newly minted Camp Average fans into a frenzy.

"You get a headband!" he yelled, tossing the one in his hand. Then he grabbed another from a batch encircling his left arm and threw it, too. "And *you* get a headband!"

Mack yanked on his own, pulling his mass of messy hair back and out of his face, and looked to the court to cheer on his team.

After Nicole got fouled in the act of shooting, she nailed two free throws to tie the game at 10–10. But nothing she or anyone else on her line did from there could pull them ahead, and Roundrock quickly went back up by four with baskets on consecutive trips.

Then Mack and everyone else in the gym watched as the two teams traded blows:

PUNCH: Shona made a baseline jump shot.

COUNTERPUNCH: Slamar, who hadn't sat yet and seemed like he might play the whole game, made a hook shot in the lane.

PUNCH: Roundrock's point guard stole the ball on the inbounds play.

COUNTERPUNCH: Darnell and Diana trapped the point guard on the sideline and stole it back.

PUNCH: After working the shooting clock down, Gavin drained a three-pointer from the left wing.

COUNTERPUNCH: Roundrock's shooting guard pulled up for three on a fast break just before the first-quarter buzzer.

At the quarter break, the score was 19–15 for Roundrock.

"Sorry, guys," Gavin said. "That was my check."

"No apologies." Nicole put her hand on her linemate's shoulder. "We'll get 'em in the third."

But Mack knew Nicole pretty well, and he could tell she was worried.

As Makayla's line took the court to start the second quarter, Mack heard a chant start up from the stands.

"When I say 'Camp,' you say 'Average!'" Pat shouted. "CAMP ..."

"AVERAGE!" shrieked their legion of fans, now about fifty members strong.

"Who are we?"

"AVERAGE!"

"What are we?"

"AVERAGE!"

On the bench, Mack winced. "I never really heard it like this before," he told Miles, "but at a certain point, this chant gets a little insulting."

The team manager smirked without taking his eyes from the court.

"What?" Mack frowned.

"You know who you sound like, right?"

Mack thought for a second. Then his eyes bugged out. Miles meant Winston. "Don't even think that!" he blurted. "I love this chant! It's the best chant ever!"

"If you say so," Miles chuckled, notching a rebound for Makayla on his spreadsheet.

After a Roundrock three pushed the lead to a game-high seven points, Camp Average answered with a bucket and a defensive stop. By the time Andre's line took the court, the score was 26–23.

"Let's go, Nelson!" someone shouted from the stands.

Nelson blushed, evidently embarrassed at the extra level of notoriety, but Andre patted him on the back.

"You got this, New Money," he encouraged.

Once the shift started, Nelson looked like he didn't even want it. Instead of hunting for the ball, he high-tailed it for the corner of the court, ready to take only catch-and-shoot threes.

The strategy had the positive effect of opening up the court for the other four players, and they took advantage by matching Roundrock basket for basket. But Mack couldn't be sure whether Nelson was trusting his gut or simply avoiding the inevitable decision-making that came with catching the ball.

In the final seconds of the quarter, things began to slip away. Slamar hit a jumper from eighteen feet to put Roundrock up five. Then he got a quick steal and nailed a three-pointer before the buzzer.

Mack watched Nelson hang his head as he slumped toward the bench.

Score at the half: 35–27, Roundrock.

CHAPTER
29

"CAPTAINS GOTTA FINISH
THE GAME"

"Slamar's killing us!" Andre raged as he and his team-mates huddled up around the bench at halftime. "Miles, how many points does he have?"

All eyes turned to the manager and his laptop.

"Oh, you don't need to know that," he said. "But I could tell you who's winning the offensive-rebounding battle. It's—"

"Miles ..." Mack pushed.

"He's got twenty-one."

"That's over half their points!" Andre shouted. "We have to find a way to slow him down."

"What if we send two defenders at him every time he touches the ball?" Wi-Fi offered.

"But that would give them a four-on-three every pos-session!"

"Makayla has had the most success defending him," Andre said. "She could play two shifts this half."

"And who would you suggest sits for her? Me?" Dillon asked.

"I didn't mean you!"

"Then who did you mean?" Diana piled on. "Which one of us do you think shouldn't be playing?"

Brian and Tamara parted their players and pushed to the center of the huddle.

"Rockets!" Tamara shouted. "Keep your cool! You don't decide who plays or sits or how we defend their star player. That's our job."

Brian took a deliberate deep breath. Watching him closely, the rest of the team followed suit. "We're down, but we're far from out," he said. "And we've got ideas on our Slamar problem, so listen up."

Seemingly seconds later, the ref called for the two teams to return to the court. Mack adjusted his headband and had just taken a couple of steps onto the court when Brian grabbed him by the back of his shirt.

"Hold up," Brian said. "You, Nicole, and Makayla are moving to the fourth shift."

Mack turned and stared at his coach, trying to process what he'd just heard.

"We're switching things up," Brian continued. "Dillon's running with the first line in your place."

At that moment, Dillon passed between them.

"Wait!" Mack grabbed his teammate by the shoulder. He realized he didn't know what to say. "Um … thanks?"

"For what?" Dillon shrugged. "You lent me a shirt, so we're cool. Besides, captains gotta finish the game."

The two players fist-bumped.

"Just watch out for alley-oop passes," Mack said. "They come out of nowhere."

Dillon joined Mack's usual linemates on the hardwood. Then he inbounded the ball to Wi-Fi, kicking off the final sixteen minutes of the tournament.

Wi-Fi tore down the court, drew defenders, and pitched the ball to Omar, who banked in a short jump shot.

"Too easy!" shouted the Roundrock head coach, showing frustration for the first time.

Wi-Fi and Omar hounded the inbounds pass. But when the point guard caught the ball, they let him dribble it up unimpeded.

"Come on!" Laker shouted from the stands. "Pressure!"

As the players dropped into defensive position in their own end, though, each took a spot on the court instead of a specific check.

"A zone," breathed Pat. "They're running a zone defense."

Three Camp Average players covered the three-point line and two dropped back to the edge of the painted area—a 3-2 formation.

Slamar held the ball at the top of the key as Wi-Fi dropped into his defensive stance in front of him. The Roundrock star surveyed the court and noticed something off, but he didn't figure out what it was until he tossed the ball to the wing.

When he cut away, Wi-Fi didn't stick with him.

"Run the zone offense!" yelled Slamar.

His teammates darted around the court, trying to remember their assignments. Meanwhile, the Camp Average players held their ground.

"Watch the baseline!" Wi-Fi yelled.

Slamar ran underneath the hoop as the ball swung from one side of the court to the other, but a defender picked him up no matter where he went.

The shot clock ticked down to one second. Roundrock's point guard heaved up a desperation three, which clanged off the rim and bounced up over the backboard.

TWEET!

"Rockets' ball!" the ref yelled.

The crowd screamed for the underdogs. On the bench, Mack cheered along, amazed at how their weeks-old sabotage plan had become a strategic advantage.

247

"I can't believe they're running a zone!" Pat shouted behind him. "This was practically my idea!"

But it wasn't *one* zone. Just when the Roundrock players thought they'd figured out the 3-2 configuration, Wi-Fi gave a hand signal—his thumbs and index fingers combining to make a rectangle—and the zone shifted to a box-and-one. That meant four players set up at the corners of the painted area, and one designated man-to-man defender—in this case, Omar—clung to Slamar wherever he went.

Recognizing the switch, Pat grabbed Laker by the upper arm and squeezed. "This is the nerdiest thing I've ever been excited about in my life!" he roared.

Slamar grew more and more frustrated as Camp Average's self-described "guarding guard" denied him the ball. And when a teammate tried to force it to him, Omar easily tapped it away, kicking off a Camp Average fast break that ended in a layup.

The two points brought Camp Average within four, just in time for the next shift change.

Nicole's line went into the game without her—like Mack, she'd been moved to the finishing five. With Bea in her place, the linemates put a full game's worth of defensive intensity into their four minutes of court time, never letting Roundrock extend the lead—but they also couldn't shrink it.

Mia subbed in for Makayla to start the fourth quarter. The move left the line lacking in size, and it hurt them on Roundrock's first possession. Slamar clanged a jumper off the back of the rim, but he followed his shot, grabbed his own rebound, and put in a layup to bring the lead to six.

"Who's gonna rebound?" said Makayla from the bench.

Sitting a few spots away, Mack watched Elijah—the line's point guard, not by choice but height—narrow his eyes. He dribbled the ball up, milked close to thirty seconds off the shot clock, then hit Ana with a tough-angled bounce pass that led to an easy basket.

But he wasn't done. Camp Average switched to man-to-man defense and kept Roundrock out of the paint, forcing a long desperation jump shot that spilled out of the hoop.

A scrum of forwards, including Mia and Luis, leapt in to corral the ball. But the smallest player on the court came away with it, elbows up to keep his opponents at bay.

"Number one!" Elijah shouted, stirring the Camp Average bench and the team's supporters into a frenzy.

A minute later, Kristi forced a Roundrock turnover and Mia made a hook shot in the lane to make the score 53–51 at the four-minute mark of the fourth quarter.

"Time out!" Brian called, sapping the players on the court of the adrenaline that had carried them through the hardest shift of their lives.

They jogged to the bench and into the arms of their teammates, cueing Mack, Andre, Nicole, Makayla, and Nelson—the final line of the game.

Tamara brought the five together, and the rest of the players gathered around them.

"It's simple, guys. Half a quarter left, down by two," she said. "You know they're good. But you're fresher than they are. You can do this."

Mack looked at his linemates. Each had a steely expression of focus.

"No more zones. Just all-out full-court press and man-to-man pressure," the coach continued. "See if you can run their legs off."

"Everybody in!" Brian shouted.

They all squished together to get their hands on the pile. "One, two, three ..."

"AVERAGE!" they shouted.

The final five took the court, their legs like coiled springs. Mack inbounded the ball to Nicole, who whipped a pass to Andre, who dribbled into the lane and dropped a pass back for Makayla. She put the ball up over her defender, and it banked off the glass into the hoop.

Tie game.

"YESSSS!" Pat shouted, along with the Camp Average cheering section.

But an expert underhanded scoop shot from the Roundrock shooting guard got the lead back to two.

"NOOOOO!" Pat cried.

As the seconds ticked down, Camp Average pressed hard, hoping to eke out as many shots as possible. But Roundrock did everything they could to slow the pace and conserve energy, breaking the press with sharp passes and draining the shot clock once they'd reached the frontcourt.

With less than a minute remaining and Camp Average still down two points, Roundrock hunted for an open shot for their best player. A bucket wouldn't officially seal the deal for the favorites, but it would make a win for the underdogs highly unlikely.

Slamar ran along the baseline through two screens, earning just enough daylight to catch a pass from the wing. As Makayla raced to catch up, he spun and faded backward, shooting a fall-away jumper …

And missed.

Mack leapt and pulled down the rebound. Just twenty seconds remained as he heaved the ball to Nicole, who whipped it forward.

Nelson caught the ball a foot outside the three-point line and came to a two-foot jump stop to avoid bowling over his defender, who was somehow both low enough to guard against the dribble and up in his grill at the same time.

"Let's go, Nelson!" Laker shouted from the stands.

It was a moment of reckoning. Nelson had a handful of options, but infinite variations on them. He could shoot with a hand in his face. He could put the ball on the floor with his right or left hand. He could force a pass to Andre or Nicole, who were both running up the left wing.

One thing he couldn't do was wait too long.

The gym was nearly shaking as supporters of both teams screamed encouragement.

Trailing the play, Mack streaked down the right side of the floor. He watched Nelson glance quickly back at him, then shift his weight for a pass to Andre, whose defender was blanketing him.

Oh no, Mack thought.

"I'm with you"—he felt something hit him in the chest—"New Money?!"

The ball was suddenly in his hands. Nelson had faked a pass one way then executed a no-look shovel pass. No hesitation. No second-guessing. And definitely no Magic 8 Ball.

"Oooh!" yelled his fans in the bleachers.

Thanks to his teammate's quick thinking, Mack now had a wide-open lane. He dribbled down it, drawing both Andre's and Nicole's defenders.

He passed the ball to Andre, who sent it on to Nicole, who was open in the left corner. With five seconds on the clock, she released a high-arcing three-point shot, snapping her wrist and holding her follow-through.

All noise ceased.

Mack watched the ball spin backward ever so slightly as it rose through the air, seemingly the only thing in the gym in motion. Then it angled back down, falling faster at a sharp angle …

And dropped through the rim, popping the net back up in its wake.

SWISH.

The crowd erupted, cheering Nicole's incredible clutch shot.

The score: 58–57, Camp Average.

Later that night, Mack would search his vocabulary for the perfect, most profound words to describe the moment, but what came out of his mouth at the time was anything but.

"AHHHHHHHHHHH!" he screamed, his arms flaring and eyes bugging out.

"AHHHHHHHHHHH!" screamed the other four Camp Average players on the court.

But the game wasn't over. With two seconds left, Slamar grabbed the ball, stepped out of bounds, and whipped it to his point guard fifteen feet away. Mack and Makayla chased him, arms in the air, as he turned and heaved the ball sidearm toward the Camp Average hoop just before the final buzzer sounded.

The ball had a one-in-a-million shot of going in.

But it did, slamming home at amazing speed.

THUNK.

Final score: 60–58, Roundrock.

The applause for Camp Average abruptly ceased as cheers for their opponents burst forth, like a DJ pulling a record off one turntable while simultaneously cranking the volume on another.

The Roundrock players and their fans rushed to center court, leaving the Camp Average five standing alone in one end.

"Oh," said Makayla matter-of-factly.

"Huh," said Nelson.

Mack put his arms around Andre's and Nicole's shoulders, which were slumped in defeat, but then he heard a rumbling and thought the roof was coming down.

He turned and saw a strange sight. Their fans—the fans of the losing team, all of them in bright orange headbands and with crazed looks on their faces—were rushing the court, too.

"That was awesome!" Special K screamed as a horde of faithful spectators mobbed them.

"You were great!" shouted Laker.

"And they were fantastic!" said Cassie, catching her brother in a bear hug.

"Incredible!" added Mike.

"They should skip high school and go straight to the pros!" Pat exalted.

"Totally!" Spike agreed.

"Guys … ?" Mack asked from the center of a jumping crowd.

"But that was amazing! *You guys* were amazing!" Pat said. "No joke!"

The Camp Average players on the bench looked at their coaches, who shrugged their shoulders and rushed the court, too. Pretty soon there was no one left on the sidelines. Everybody in the gym—players, fans, coaches, organizers, refs—was on the court, dancing and jumping, shouting and screaming, high-fiving and hand-shaking.

When the celebration finally died down, the fans climbed back into the stands, and Candace returned to center court with her microphone.

After lining the teams up as she had earlier, she awarded the tournament trophy to Roundrock's coaches and the MVP award to Slamar, who, despite not hitting the game-winner, had done more than enough to earn it. Then she pulled gold medals from a cardboard box and placed one around the neck of each Roundrock player.

"Wait!" Andre said. "If they get gold, that means we get—"

"Silver," Mack said, watching Candace pull a second set of medals out of the box. Then he looked up at Pat, who was watching the organizer with wide eyes. "We get silver."

EPILOGUE

"I MADE A DEAL"

The basketball players received the Camp Average version of a hero's welcome upon their return to camp: chili dogs in the mess hall. It was easily the least healthy meal of the summer, but with Winston gone, no one complained.

Still, Mack felt something was off. He received so many backslaps and handshakes that he started to wonder if his campmates thought they'd actually won the final.

"So what was it like?" Hassan asked when the players finally found their way through cheering throngs to take a seat with their food.

Seeing an opportunity to set the record straight, Mack regaled him with the story—from the bus fiasco to the buzzer-beater—and his counselor listened in rapt attention.

"Sorry you couldn't be there to see it," Mack said when he finished.

"Oh, we saw it," Hassan answered excitedly. "They streamed the tournament on the Swish City website, and

Cheryl set up a viewing station on a big screen in the field house. That last shot was *bonkers.*"

Mack frowned. "So wait—if everyone actually *watched* us lose, why does this feel like a victory celebration?"

Hassan did a double take. "Are you kidding?" he asked earnestly.

"No?" Mack answered.

"You've gotta be kidding!"

"I'm not! I don't get it!"

Hassan furrowed his brow, studying Mack's bewildered expression. Then he smiled. "Nice try, Mack. But you've got some work to do before you get to Pat's level with the practical jokes."

Hassan picked up his tray and left for the garbage can while Mack looked around, wild-eyed in confusion. Then his gaze settled on Andre, who had evidently been listening in from across the table. He was smiling, too.

"We did our best." Andre shrugged. "And I think they could all see that."

Before Mack could reply, Miles jumped in.

"And our best turned out to be way better than anyone expected it would be."

Pat leaned in. "And it was weird."

"*So* weird," Cassie added, sliding onto Mack's chair. "Plus, my brother was really good."

"*Stop,*" Nelson pleaded, dropping into the chair next to her.

"She's right, though," said Nicole, falling in next to Andre with Makayla at her side. "You all were."

"Just one thing bugged me," Makayla added. "No one chanted, 'We're number two'—even though we actually were. I mean, don't you guys love doing that?"

Andre threw up his hands. "What do you mean 'you guys'? Aren't you one of us?" he asked as the conversation spilled over into vigorous trash talk.

Mack looked at his friends, now tightly huddled around him, and he saw them the way he guessed his campmates had. They weren't laser-focused athletic assassins like the kids at Killington or Roundrock, but they competed like crazy. They weren't bullies like the players from BC Select, but they always stood up for themselves and those they cared about. They were the type of kids to attend a second-tier sports camp because that's where their friends were. And he was so glad he could say he was one of them.

They're not average, he thought, finally getting it. *They're* Average.

The players roused themselves and left the mess hall for a loud and unruly board game night in the lodge. Afterward, when the dice and checkers and instruction books had all been accounted for and put away, counselors gathered up their charges to head to the cabins for lights-out.

But Mack still had one thing he wanted to do.

"Short detour?" he asked Brian and Hassan.

Mack led his cabinmates around the far side of the office and down the hill toward the beach.

"Uh, Mack?" Brian said. "We're not going swimming."

Mack didn't reply. He just veered away from the waterfront path onto another one. The one that led to the camp director's cabin.

Before Brian or Hassan could protest, Mack bounded up the steps and opened the door, his cabinmates at his heels.

The boys spilled inside and stood in awe of the emptiness and quiet of the large room. Winston hadn't taken the furniture or the pictures on the wall, but nothing of him remained. For two summers he had been an unpredictable, unrelenting storm cloud over the camp—low and dark and full of thunder—and now he was gone.

No one spoke. Finally, Mack said what they were all thinking.

"Next summer's going to be different."

They all nodded—except Andre, who seemed to crumple like he'd been punched in the stomach.

"What?" Mack asked.

His friend's eyes danced around under the lowered brim of his A's cap, seemingly looking for a way out of the question. Finally, his shoulders dropped. "I won't be here to see it," he said weakly.

The words hit everyone in the room like a sledge-hammer, but no one said a word. This was a two-person conversation, and they all knew it.

"Where will you be?" Mack asked with a steely voice.

"I made a deal," Andre answered. "For the bus."

Mack stared, waiting for him to continue.

"Deets. He told me at the baseball tournament that they had a spot for me. I thought I could use that."

Miles sat down hard on Winston's old couch. "A 'spot for you,' not a 'pot of stew'!" he whispered cryptically.

Mack's gaze never left his friend's face. "Where will you be next summer?"

Tears welled in Andre's eyes. "Killington," he said.